PUNK OFF!!!

CHRISTINE SLANZ

FOR PUNKS EVERYWHERE

PROLOGUE

"Look, honey, you better pull those panties and do those squats or I'll have a couple of the fellas come in and help you."

Those are the words no woman wants to hear, but I heard them, and I hope it never happens again. As a Young Libertarian, I think body cavity searches should never happen to anyone, ever. My oldest friend, Adnan Kashmir, says, "Those body cavity searches are just a way for the pigs to get their rocks off." I had to get naked in front of a stranger, which is always sort of embarrassing, and then the stranger tells me to squat so that if I have a gun hidden inside my vag, it will clatter down onto the floor.

It's really not that awful. I haven't been traumatized for life; I don't have PTSD or need shrinks and meds. But those who have had to squat are unlikely to forget it anytime soon—if ever.

Having to squat isn't physically painful, but it *is* humiliating and degrading. I haven't had to go to a support group and stand up to say, "My name's Christine, and this big ugly woman in a blue uniform told me to get naked and squat..." But was it really necessary for those bullies to humiliate me that way?

This is the story of how I ended up in that predicament.

It's also the story of how I was president of my high school's Young Libertarians. I had already been accepted at Stanford and was slathering over becoming a wonderfully overpaid professional person upon graduation. I truly believed that we have control over our own lives. Well, that's bullshit. I know now that our scripts are written for us even before we are born, and we simply follow those scripts. It's just our egos that tell us we are the masters of our own fates. My belief in fatalism happened because of my weird, strange journey that culminated in a cold, overlit room in Chicago where I pulled my panties and did my squats...

CHAPTER 1

The terms *Young Libertarian* and *strip search* seldom go together. Libertarians say there shouldn't be cavity searches, nor should there be cops or border guards. In fact, there probably should not be borders.

I wasn't born a libertarian; I was just born me. But I do know some things about genes, and I know that I was born a Spurl, which accounts for the crazy woman in me.

Here's what I'm getting at: I joined the Young Libertarians so I could help control myself whenever I became a Spurl Girl and acted out. Well, that's sort of true, anyway.

The main reason I joined the Young Libertarians was Senator Ewoldt. Wizard had helped with Ewoldt's election bid. We called our classmate Wizard because she was smarter than most of our teachers. She brought along a couple of other people, and I went to campaign headquarters, I suppose, only because they were going there and I wanted to see what it was all about. The moment I eyeballed Sam Raney collating documents, I knew I was in love. He had those fresh-faced *GQ* looks that made me drool.

I marched right up and started collating with him.

"New volunteer?" he asked. His smile was so big, bright and perfect that I wondered if his teeth were real.

"New and exciting." Boredom and loneliness had

brought me to the Libertarian Party. Infatuation kept me there.

Ewoldt was someone I could easily get behind. The Democrats and GOP made me nauseous. They represented the two sides of the big-government coin. Ewoldt had a personality that could fill a ballroom. He was young, under forty, and when he spoke of what he thought and felt, well, I could practically hear the swells of "The Battle Hymn of the Republic." He believed that America would be far better off if we returned to the values that Thomas Jefferson embraced back in 1776.

The only time I ever took crap for working in that campaign office was when I told Adnan about it. He didn't believe in politics at all; "I am opposed to all institutional and authoritarian power," he'd told me. He dressed in black every day, and said he was in mourning for the human race.

"You joined the Young Libertarians?" he said. "Christine, what *is* your problem?"

"You should meet Ewoldt," I said. "He's the man!"

"He's a politician. He's full of shit."

"*You're* full of shit."

"Yes," he retorted, "but at least I don't deny it."

Adnan and I could speak to each other that way and neither would take offense because we had known each other almost since birth. We had spent countless hours in the playpen together, smacking each other silly while our mothers visited over tea in the next room. As far back as I could remember, Adnan had been in my life. She knew as much about me as anyone could—but the Spurl in me had remained a secret.

Adnan went out and volunteered for the Independent candidate, some guy whose name I couldn't pronounce. He wanted to legalize all hard drugs and lower the drinking age to sixteen. Good luck with that, I thought.

The Independent candidate ran out of money and skedaddled. Ewoldt won, mostly because the voters considered him the most harmless of those seeking office. I was addicted. Power and success are the most powerful drugs imaginable.

Here's what kind of *chutzpah* Adnan has: When Ewoldt won, he threw a victory party on a cruise ship. Adnan, who had toiled for one of the losers, insisted that I take him along as my date.

"Nix," I said. "You worked for Ewoldt's competitor. Go to the Independent guy's party—oh, I forgot; your guy lost, so he's not throwing any party."

But Adnan wasn't having any of it. He had already decided that he was going to that party with me, period. It had been that way all our lives—we would do things his way, and I would go along with it, period. If I didn't like it, tough titties.

He had started dressing like Johnny Rotten by that time, so his studded leathers and spiky hair went over poorly at that party.

For me, that cruise was disastrous. Wizard kept staring at as if Adnan the punk were a baboon that had escaped from the zoo. He reviled Ewoldt to everyone who would listen. Our friend Carsten was there, too, and Adnan started in on him about this and that. Then Adnan flipped him off in front of a dozen other guests.

"Is he your boyfriend, Christine?" Sam Raney asked me.

"Hardly."

"But it looks like the two of you came here together."

I shrugged. "We've known each other forever. I felt sorry for him. He doesn't get out much, so I brought him along."

Later on that evening I caught Sam making out with some chick in an isolated part of the ship. He seemed to get turned on by seeing Adnan flipping someone the bird. If so, I would have asked Adnan to punch me out in front of Sam.

Adnan was one of those people who would surprise you just as you concluded that you knew him and could predict his behavior. Wizard, who didn't like surprises or volatile people, tiptoed around Adnan.

What about Sam? Well, I don't think I was really that infatuated with him after all. I guess my Spurl genes were just asserting themselves.

Why, I asked myself, did I let Adnan boss me around? Yes, he was pushy and temperamental, but he wasn't John Gotti or Eddie Nash. I simply had to say no and mean it. But I let him have his own way.

Strangely, I had a huge assertiveness issue with Adnan, as if my backbone had turned to mush. I knew I didn't find him attractive in a physical or romantic way. He was as far from being my type as a guy could get. I didn't go for spiky hair, black apparel and grim outlooks. I also thought punk rock was just so much mindless noise; he adored bands with names like Swarm and Colostomy.

Every time he started to sass me and I got ready to

tell him off, I remembered the day when his father and mine went off to work and, as the two men stood side by side on the subway platform, Adnan's dad dropped dead from a heart attack.

That experience freaked out my dad as much as it did Adnan's family. My dad, fearing he would be next to die from some sort of stress-related disorder, quit his Financial District job and bought a corner store in our neighborhood.

So, maybe as my way of telling Adnan how very sorry I was for his loss, I let him have things pretty much his own way whenever we went somewhere or did something together. I thought, To lose your dad so early and suddenly in life. It really sucks.

CHAPTER 2

I bet the idea of high school Libertarians sounds pretty lame—a bunch of spoiled brats who weep for the underprivileged because that seems to be the fashionable thing to do. But our intentions were actually honorable. We knew that our country and its government were dominated by Democrats and Republicans and often we had difficulty telling them apart. So we wanted to learn as much as we could about libertarianism and what it might look like if the Libertarian Party controlled the presidency and congress. We didn't consider ourselves superior to anyone; we were just exploring libertarianism as a way of improving America. I know that my Spurl genes hated my libertarian beliefs, and that was a good thing.

Adnan kept trying to make a nihilist of me.

"The Young Libertarians is just a school thing," I reminded him. "It's harmless. It means zilch."

"I would rather see you as a crackhead than a Young Libertarian. Anyway, I think you're a phony libertarian. Deep down inside, you want a cushy job that pays big bucks."

I shrugged. "Maybe. But is there something wrong with that? Whether you're a libertarian or a nihilist, you have to get a job and earn a paycheck. Therefore, shouldn't you get the best job you can?"

Adnan put his hands together in prayer, closed his

eyes and lifted his face to the sky. "Oh, Almighty Greenback, come to me and compensate me for the disappointments in my personal life…" Adnan had been in the drama club for a while. He quit because he and the drama instructor had some disagreements over minor things such as how to act, sing and dance. "The best things in life are free," he added. "Fun, poetry, music, love…"

"You can have all that stuff and be rich, too."

He waved me off. "Forget about fast cars and designer clothing. Think about ideas and culture, art and philosophy."

I nodded. "My philosophy is, art can be a great investment. Picassos can fetch huge money at auctions."

I enjoyed teasing him. He was more than tough enough to take it. As Adnan and I spoke in the school cafeteria, he stood with one boot on the floor and the other on the seat of the bench, and he did so in such a way as to make it very difficult for others to pass behind him.

When one of the track-and-field boys tried to get by and had to struggle for several for several moments past Adnan's bulk, the jock muttered "Faggot" in a voice so quiet that I could scarcely hear him. But Adnan heard him, too, and instantly fired an elbow into the guy's lunch tray, which clattered onto the floor along with its owner's meal.

The jock scowled. "You fuckin'—"

Adnan scowled back. "Better step back, dude."

The jock raised a fist, but then thought better of it. Adnan feared nobody, would mix it up with every antagonist who came at him. The jock might win the fight but would risk losing a couple of teeth or a testicle. He backed off and headed to the boys' can to wash the lunch off his shirt.

Adnan turned to me. "As I was saying…"

He didn't simply like music. He embraced it as his religion, to the extent that he had one. He believed that punk rock held the answers to life's largest and most vexing questions; or maybe punk's answer was, "Fuck it all. Life's questions are meaningless."

"You care a lot about punk rock. I don't. I care about other things. You should respect that. How many times have we talked about the importance of tolerance for others?"

"I would accept your rejection of punk," he said, "if you actually *knew* what you were rejecting. When it comes to punk, you don't even know what you don't know."

Well, how can I argue with a person who has a clever retort for everything?

Fortunately, I had another friend who'd already forgotten more than I had ever learned. Wizard knew more about the Internet—and most other things— than anyone else I knew. Wizard figured out that Adnan was the author of one of the more popular blogs.

"How do you know that he writes that blog?" I asked.

"Because I know."

"Come on, just tell me."

She shrugged. "I checked out the traffic that was being routed through the school's server."

"Simple as that?"

She nodded. "Things are fairly visible when you know what you're looking for." Then, "On that cruise? He said that most of the food was so full of cholesterol that he was amazed nobody dropped dead of a heart attack."

Wizard was right, which was how she had acquired her nickname. But why would a computer star like her, so used to deep thinking and big ideas, spend so much time reading Adnan's blog?

"You got a thing for him?"

Wizard blushed. "Ask me something else."

"So the truth comes out," I said. "Infatuation is not a new thing in the world. It's not something to be ashamed of, either."

"I wish he didn't make himself look so freaky all the time."

"Wiz, you're going to be Ruler of the Universe one day. Choose your friends carefully and marry the handsomest man in Hollywood."

I didn't believe that Wizard was in love with Adnan. All brainy little wimps seem to find the Adnans of this world exciting and dangerous. Myself, I had never thought of Adnan as anything but a person and friend. His black clothing and dark soul turned me off, and the only reason I considered him my friend was that I had known him as far back as I could remember.

"Adnan looks like something from a Tim Burton movie," said Ling as she read through a copy of *Forbes* magazine.

"Shut up and mind your own business," I told her. I could rag on Adnan all I wanted, but would defend him against all others. I had to agree, though; Adnan went through life as a character, not a person. I had trouble perceiving him as a guy who would go out on dates and make out with girls. I also had difficulty seeing Wizard as a girl who might be of interest to guys, with her lack of curves and her big glasses.

"There's someone who likes you," I said to Adnan. "Wanna know who?"

"Nope."

"Gonna tell you anyway."

"Keep it to yourself."

"It's Wizard."

He frowned. "Who?"

I gave him a few details, then he nodded.

"That skinny, brainy chick who looks like an owl. How come she's picking on me?"

I laughed. "She's not picking on you. She's just very interested in you."

He shuddered. "She's not a chick. She's, like, a walking computer." He paused. "I would never date a genius."

"Well, maybe she's working up the nerve to ask you out. If that happens, be nice and just say no thanks. You don't have be a jerk and make fun of her."

"No jerk here," he said. "Truth is, I guess I feel honored. I want to interface my hard drive with her floppy function."

"Jerk."

Want another example of what big balls my friend Adnan has? While mocking one of my friends, he asked me to tutor his friend Chris Culver, who was slipping a little bit in history.

"Nix to that," I said. "If you have so little concern for Wizard's feelings, I have no concern for Culver's history grade."

He sneered. The look on his face was so menacing that my heart. "You don't like him because he's queer."

"His sexual orientation," I shot back, "is none of my concern. I don't like him because he's totally convinced that he's superior to the rest of humankind."

"Well, maybe he *is*. He's, like, too gifted. He's been tested and everything. Sometimes gifted people have poor social skills."

"If he's so gifted, how come he needs my help?"

"Because he gets bored easily with things he considers irrelevant, and to him history is meaningless."

"Culver's not even good at being queer. When did you last see him with a boyfriend?"

"When did *you* last have a boyfriend?" Adnan retorted. "If you need a date on Saturday night, it's usually me."

I wanted to say, 'If you hadn't been such an *asshole* on that cruise, Sam Raney might have been my guy by now.' But I said nothing.

"You don't understand how difficult it is for Culver," Adnan said. "They forced him into this 'accelerated' program where he has to take 'honors' courses. It's not up to him at all."

I nodded. I knew about Culver. When he was in first grade, they tested him and measured his IQ at close to 200. The school board called him a genius, a label that over time became a monkey on the kid's back. I supposed that nobody stopped to think that the almost-200 IQ didn't necessarily mean all that much. Culver was a smart enough boy, but was he going from high school to MIT or Caltech and dazzle the world's intellectual elite? Nix to that. Whenever he tried to transfer out of the accelerated program, they refused to honor his request because the 'normal' program would just bore him.

"Hard luck," I said.

"He needs your help. You're a stud at history—Johnson Scholarship, Stanford wants you—"

"Yeah, OK, I'll do it." I wasn't sure why. I was in my senior year, up to my butt in examinations and needing to maintain my high GPA so Stanford wouldn't revoke its offer of admission. I would be donating my independent-study blocks to tutoring someone who believed he had nothing to learn from me.

"I understand you're having some issues with history," I said to him.

Culver checked me out. "Your hair is too long. It's too frizzy and it doesn't look natural."

My hair was naturally blonde and frizzy. I liked it long; I was vain about my long blonde locks.

"Your nose is much too big," he added.

"So is your mouth," I retorted.

He stared at my chest for a few long moments. "Your girls are too small—have you thought of wearing a padded bra?"

"Let's not get personal."

Culver nodded. "OK. So…which part of history do you need help with?"

That was his attitude. He was helping me, not vice versa.

Evidently, I was the one who had trouble keeping straight the facts of history. Hour after hour, day after day, I explained U.S. history to him till my face turned blue. At times I felt as if I were talking to myself.

"Making any progress?" Adnan asked me daily.

"Not much," I replied, and the look he gave me said, *It's your fault.*

I kept on with Culver. I learned some things about myself: my butt was too big, I had no fashion sense at all and my nose was one of the great wonders of the world. Alas, he learned very little about history.

I stumbled onto a breakthrough. Culver loved movies, so I told him to download some videos about American history. Hollywood tells stories much better than textbooks do, and after Culver finished watching a handful of them, he said, "Now I know more about that shit than you do."

"So you'll be ready to take the test?"

He nodded.

We ended up taking the same test at the same table at the same time in our school's cafeteria. We sat across from each other, and I really shouldn't have cared about the panicked look in his eyes as he looked down at his blank blue test booklet that needed to be filled with his handwritten answers. Had he forgotten it all so soon?

I wanted to haul off and punch him out. All those hours of my own time I'd spent with him, as a personal favor to Adnan! All of it for zero!

So I did the one thing I knew I must not do. I mouthed, *Culver! Remember the videos!*

Then I felt the cold, hard hand clamp down on my shoulder.

CHAPTER 3

Fortunately, Mr. Schloss liked me. One of the good things about the Young Libertarians club was that the teachers admired our hard work and dedication. We had gotten some recognition from the community and that made the school look good.

But talking during an exam? Whoo, bad stuff, man.

"Sharing answers with Chris Culver," said Mr. Schloss. "What was the thinking behind that?"

"It wasn't like that at all," I told him. "He seemed to draw a blank, so I just offered him a word of encouragement."

"So *he* was cheating, not you."

"Nobody was cheating."

"But something that looked like cheating happened in the cafeteria, and I think we all know what cheating is." Then, "You've said that he was having difficulties with history and you'd been helping him with that. In the cafeteria, he made you give him the answer and you complied. That's a huge infraction."

I shook my head. "But he didn't make me give him an answer. In fact—" I had enough sense to shut up then and avoid getting myself into trouble over this matter.

We stayed quiet for a few moments. Then he said, "You better tell me what I need to hear, Christine. As I said, a major infraction was committed. The guilty party must be punished. You're a smart young lady who can really go places in this world, so don't jeopardize your future. If you were innocent in this matter, you must acknowledge that right now."

I nodded. I understood. Mr. Schloss didn't want to get me into any trouble. He wanted an excuse to punish Culver. I guess the principal didn't like queers very much.

I empathized with Culver. I really did. After all, here was this kid who started high school with a reputation for being a mental giant, and maybe it would have been OK if he really had been some sort of genius, which he certainly was not, although in most areas he was academically gifted (hardly the same thing as being a genius). Mostly, what it did was proclaim to the world, "This is Chris Culver—he is *different*." Plus, by high school it became clear to him—and everyone else—that he was gay, which made him that much more of an outsider.

"It's kind of you to tutor another student and use your intelligence to help him," Mr. Schloss was saying. "But you must remember that you're an adult now, and your actions, as well as the people you associate with."

Mr. Schloss just wanted me to incriminate Culver so I could walk out of that office unscathed and he could begin the process of expelling the queer kid.

I felt *her* inside me then—Spurl—and the stiffening of my features was something she, not I, controlled.

I had spent the past while as a Young Libertarian,

talking about things like character, integrity and honor, but my *real* interests were Stanford University and making out with Sam Raney in the backseat of his car, assuming he had one. But this deal right here, Spurl seemed to be saying, was the real test of my character. Could I respect myself if I fucked over Culver by accusing the kid of cheating on an examination?

"I didn't cheat, Mr. Schloss. Neither did Chris Culver. Nobody cheated. There were no infractions."

His eyes narrowed. "Be careful of what you say and do, Christine. There *has* been an infraction and someone is going to be penalized. You should make sure *you* aren't the victim."

Spurl made me stand up and say, "If that is all, I need to go to my next class."

Whatever goodwill existed between us disappeared as instantly as a puff of smoke. He was doing me a huge favor and I was unwilling to accept it. He leaned forward and sad, "Don't be stupid, Miz Slanz. This whole matter could put a big black mark on your permanent academic record."

I shrugged, repeated that I had done nothing wrong, and left the office before Spurl could make me say anything hugely regrettable.

All that day I felt jinxed. Spurl, the force that had sat dormant inside of me for so long, had awakened and gotten restless. But why now, when my permanent academic record was at risk and Stanford had said, "Get your ass in here!"?

When I got home that day, I still felt full of anxiety and distress, so I slipped into my room and phoned Julie Riding, my admissions counselor at Stanford and practically sobbed as I ran it all down for het.

"No need to worry, Christine," she said. "That test means nothing to us. We've already accepted you, so as long as you get your diploma in June, we'll be seeing you in September."

I thanked her and ended our conversation, hoping that she was right about everything.

"They tell me you got busted for cheating on that test in the caf," said Ling as she sat across from me and ate her crap sandwich.

Sam Raney sat at our table, too. He looked at me with his big dark eyes. "Really, Christine? Tell us about it."

I shook my head. "I did not cheat."

"So you didn't get caught copying from the gay kid? That's what people are saying," Ling told me.

I lifted my chin. "I did nothing wrong."

"But the monitor *did* put his hand on your shoulder and take away your test booklet. Right?" Ling asked.

I nodded. "They reduced my score to zilch. But I didn't cheat, and no one cheated from me. I'm just blowing this off as one of life's unfortunate experiences."

Ling frowned. "I don't want to kick you when you're down, but Young Libertarians must have clean records if they are to serve as officers."

"That's stupid. Who came up with such a rule?"

She pointed at me.

"Well," I said, "I'll sort things out."

Just then Adnan joined us. "Hey, guys," he said as he set down his lunch tray and made himself comfortable. To Ling he said, "How are your investments going?"

Ling made a face. She didn't like him, and she certainly disliked his questions about her up-and-down portfolio in the Investors' Club, in which members used hypothetical money to buy stock in real companies.

Adnan waved at Culver and invited him to join us. Lovely, I thought. Just freakin' lovely.

Culver had a remarkable talent for making breathtakingly inappropriate remarks. As he sat at our table, he asked, "So, how did everyone do on that test we took in here?"

"You know how *I* did," I said with a sneer. "You were there. Unfortunately."

"Well, that was yummy." Ling pushed away her salad, which she'd devoured in a few bites. She probably still felt ravenous. I guessed she was anorexic; she'd made fat jokes about herself, even though she didn't weigh much more than a hundred pounds.

"You ready to go?" she asked Sam.

"Nope," he said, pointing at his half-eaten lunch.

Ling got up, pulled Sam to his feet and said, "Keep good thoughts, Christine. Hope Stanford accepts you."

"They already have."

"Sweet."

As Ling and Sam walked away, Adnan said, "I don't like that chick."

Culver said, "Her problem is that she needs to get in touch with her inner lesbian."

I nearly spat up a mouthful of Coke Zero. "Ling? She has an inner lesbian?"

He nodded. "And she represses it. That's why

she's so—"

"Heterosexual," Adnan interjected.

I pointed to a document sitting next to Adnan's lunch tray. "What's that?"

"English assignment. My topic is punk rock."

"I bet your teacher will have many hours of fun reading it," I said.

"What do *you* know about punk rock?" Culver asked.

"More than *you* know about American history," I retorted. "Adnan is the only person I know who would do a paper on the worst kind of music in human history. How can you have any respect for a band called the Sex Pistols?"

Adnan scowled at me. "Punk is much more than the Sex Pistols. My favorite punk band in all the world is an all-girl group called Swarm. That band united all punks—whatever kind of punk you were, you had to admire and respect Swarm."

"Why?" I asked.

"Because," he explained, "Swarm was the consummate punk band. Their debut album was *On the Rag*, full of enraged lyrics and crazy rants by Queen Bea, the band's sexy, tortured lead singer." He paused. "One of the most significant moments in music history was the formation of Swarm by Queen Bea and Maxie Padz. Queen Bea was born Beatrix Potter Spurl."

I swallowed hard. I felt my stomach jump.

Spurl.

CHAPTER 4

I want to tell you my life's story, so I guess it's best to start at the beginning. But I'm going to start on a day when I was about ten years old. At school we were planning a field trip to Canada and I needed to find my birth certificate. I found it—plus something I didn't expect: An adoption record. The names of the biological mother and father were Beatrix Spurl and Mark Ignas.

"What is this?" I practically shouted. "Was I adopted? Who is Beatrix Spurl? Is this a joke?"

"No joke," said Mom. "We adopted you shortly after you were born. Even though we're not your birth parents, we still love you and you are *our* child."

"So that explains why my nose is so big and yours aren't," I said. "All this time, I've thought you dropped me on my face or something."

Dad threw his arm around Mom and said, "Your mother and I love you very much."

"Good to know. Now, who *are* Beatrix Spurl and Mark Ignas?"

"Your birth mother," Dad said with the utmost care, "was a confused young lady who wasn't yet ready for parenthood. She conceived with a young man who similarly wasn't prepared to assume the duties of raising a child. So they unselfishly allowed us to give you everything they could not."

I sighed. "That still doesn't answer my question." But I could have asked them a hundred specific questions about my biological parents and their answers would have left me feeling even sadder and more confused.

I got my documentation in order and went to Canada with my class. Like Linda Blair in *The Exorcist*, I had become someone else, sort of. Spurl acted out and ruined everyone's good time.

"Christine, what's happened to you?" my teacher wanted to know.

What could I say? I'd tried to be nice and get along, but Spurl felt like being a bitch and there wasn't much I could about her expect hang my head in shame.

I remember little of that trip, but have been told that I danced along the edge of an overpass as traffic roared by dozens of feet below. I sang, "This is the end, my friends," and dared them to dare me to jump to my death.

"I don't recall any of that," I said to m parents after the teachers told them about it.

"It's just as well," said Mom. "But you've got to control your impulses."

No—I had to control Spurl's impulses. But how?

I kept after my mom to give me more information about my birth parents, but she mostly just said, "She was young. So was he. It was an indiscretion. Does it really matter now?"

"Who was Mark Ignas? Was he a pretty-boy *GQ* model? What about Beatrix Spurl? How come my nose is so big?"

"I've told you all I know, Christine. You're a Slanz.

Isn't that good enough?"

So I went to the Internet and learned more than I wanted to know.

CHAPTER 5

I looked at the name on the screen a few dozen times, just to make sure I had it right.

Beatrix P. Spurl.

She had to be the one. How many other women had that name? She was my biological mother, whether I liked it or not.

Of course, I had always assumed I would learn about my biological mother, but believed my adoptive mother would spill it after I had bugged her enough.

Wow! My bio-mommy, "Queen Bea," was famous! An American musical institution, if I could believe Adnan. Her band, Swarm, had its own Website, on which Queen Bea and her princess bragged about being busted for destruction of private and public property, possession of controlled substances, gross indecency, civil disobedience. Yessir, they'd graduated at the top of their class.

Adnan spoke of Swarm's illegal exploits with the rosy glow of pride warming his cheeks. I reminded him that in another time and place, people who did what those women had done were incarcerated and even executed. He said life wasn't fair.

I had always told myself that my Spurl genes were to blame for my bad behavior. Now I knew I was right! At first I thought that having a mom who was a longtime and prominent member of show business was a kind of groovy thing, but Queen Bea seemed more a terrorist than a musician. The blood of an infamous bitch coursed through my body.

Swarm made international headlines by holding a press conference for dozens of reporters, then locking the doors for three days and keeping their hostages alive on pizza and bottled water, a la *Dog Day Afternoon*. Many assumed the band had staged the ordeal, but Swarm did three months in jail and received a stiff fine.

One time, Queen Bea suspected their business manager of ripping them off, so she rode her Harley through the glass doors of his office, then whipped out a sword and threatened to emasculate him.

My bio-mama was more than simple another rock star; she was the closest thing our culture had to a female Charles Manson. When Swarm went on tour, families locked and chained their doors, church groups demonstrated against the band and even labor unions dreaded being hired to handle the group's equipment. After Swarm released its album "Shoot the Prez," Ronald Reagan called the band "a disgrace to America." England and France refused to permit Swarm to perform in those countries as part of the band's European tour. It didn't hurt Swarm's notoriety that its leader, Queen Bea, was very close to being gorgeous. Smut peddler Larry Flynt offered her a million dollars to pose nude in *Hustler* magazine. She declined.

"Queen broke my heart," said Adnan, "when she said no to *Hustler*. I really wanted to see what her vag was like."

"A vag is a vag, I," I told him. "Seen one, seen 'em all. Trust me on this."

Swarm retired in the early 1990s, when the bitchiest band in America also became one of the richest and gave in to complacency. They inspired dozens of bands who thanked them in their album liner notes. "The Sluts learned most of what they know from Swarm," said Adnan. "The Sluts are so awesome, they could be almost as great as Brain Dead one day. But of course there will never be another Swarm."

I got more than 200,000 results when I Googled the search words "Queen Bea." Born in Ohio on July 10, 1963, she attended Miami University with the vague ambition of becoming a business manager or accountant.

So my bio-mama started out life as essentially a normal, regular gal. As a Young Libertarian, I was, in some ways, her daughter, I supposed.

Then I checked out her picture from 1985. Her shock of blonde hair and blunt stare were all punk, but she was beautiful enough to have chosen Hollywood over Swarm. Still, I could see that the blaze of rage in her eyes and the tautness of her unsmiling lips were real, and I wondered how or why such a beautiful young woman could be so full of venom. If Swarm was punk's bitchiest band, Queen was surely its bitchiest member, and had sat for that image on my screen during a day of scorching PMS.

I studied her face for some trace of family resemblance but could find nothing. After a while I heard my parents coming down the hallway so I closed Queen's image. My folks would probably be less offended if they caught me looking at kiddie porn than pictures of that Swarm bitch.

CHAPTER 6

"So I came into this world because of Queen Bea and Mark Ignas," I said as a way of making conversation. "Was he a groupie or something?"

"We don't know," said my adoptive father, "and it really doesn't matter."

"Oh, but it *does*," I retorted. "It matters to me. A lot."

My adoptive mother looked up from her crossword puzzle. "We've already had this conversation. Enough said."

The Spurl Girl in me wanted to snatch away that crossword puzzle and stuff it up Mom's butt. Instead, I helped her with it, and she told me a few things.

"Your father and I couldn't conceive, so we learned of this young woman who'd just had a baby girl—"

"That would be me."

She nodded. "She had this on-again, off-again boyfriend—"

"Mark Ignas."

She nodded again. "And parenthood just didn't fit into their plans. Punks aren't supposed to have kids. It's just uncool, I guess."

"Go on."

She shrugged. "It's hard for me to talk about because there isn't much to say. This woman—she wasn't much more than a girl in most ways—was a punk musician, not exactly our kind of people, but she had a kid even though she was still very much a kid herself, and I guess the challenges of raising a child freaked her out. So there was this stable, childless couple out there—"

"That would be you."

"Yes. And we wanted a child but couldn't have one. So, here we are."

Yes, there we were. I had gotten all the information I was going to get, and none of it made me feel any better about my birth parents or myself.

I could hardly just go on with my life, accepting Mister and Missus Slanz as my only parents and mostly ignoring the fact that Queen Bea of Swarm was my bio-mama and we would probably never meet. We *had* to meet. I *had* to get to know this woman, if only because she was rich and famous and in a position to help me—and with an obligation to help me.

Naturally, I had no way of knowing then that, because of her, I would end up in that police station pulling off my panties and doing my squats.

Like everyone else my age, I had been to countless record stores, but as soon as I stepped into our nearest megastore I felt as if everyone were looking at me, saying to each other, "There she is! The bastard daughter of Queen Bea!" I moseyed on over to the Swarm bin and pulled out a CD called *Men Are Scum*.

As I stood in line at the cash register, my cheeks

burned with embarrassment. I didn't feel that way at all about the opposite sex.

The cashier held up my purchase and smiled. "Oh! This one made me a lesbian!"

"Is that good?" I asked.

I took it home and played it on my MacBook Pro. I even put on headphones first so that my adoptive parents wouldn't be able to overhear what my birth mother did for a living back in the 1980s.

The world had few punk libertarians—the punks were nihilists and anarchists who seemed to believe in torching everything just to watch it burn. I concluded that I had no more use for them than they had for me. I listened to *Men Are Scum* in one sitting. What did I think? Well, I was no *Rolling Stone* critic, but even I could tell that Swarm made noise as opposed to playing music. Dissonant guitars, screaming vocals and monotonous drumming marked, or marred, each track. I found Queen Bea totally incomprehensible at all times—and perhaps that was the point. Our cruel, vicious world had reduced her to a screaming maniac.

I stuck *Men Are Scum* into my CD collection and did my best to forget about it.

The next day at school, I did something I thought I would never do. Over lunch, I said, "Adnan, yesterday I bought a CD of *Men Are Scum*. I listened to it from start to finish.

He sneered at me. "Liar."

I shook my head. "I'm serious."

"Your idea of music is Britney Spears, Madonna and U2."

"Not true. Aren't you always ragging on me for

listening to the same crap as everyone else? Well, I took your advice and checked Swarm out."

Adnan pursed his lips and frowned for a few moments. "So, did you love it or what?"

"Well, not as much as you do."

He shook his head. "No, you won't love Swarm at first. That's because you didn't understand it. People love mainstream pop music because it's been dumbed down so much—and *people* have been dumbed down so much—that there's nothing *not* to understand about that kind of music. But Swarm takes some getting used to. You have to listen to it a lot in order to understand what it's about."

"Why is their CD called *Men Are Scum*? I think men are OK. No worse than women."

"It's just another way of saying *people* are scum," Adnan said. "People will stop being scum when they've decided to stop being scum. Queen doesn't think that day will ever arrive, though."

I shrugged. "I guess that makes me scum, too. I don't mind, as long as I get to be Stanford scum. I guess Queen Bea's message just sails over my head."

"Too bad for you," said Adnan.

"Say, what's their song 'Drop a Deuce' about?"

"Doncha love that title?" Culver asked. He often invited himself to sit with us at lunchtime, even though we wished he would sit elsewhere. "It's about not giving a shit—literally. It's just too clever."

Adnan smiled. "The bullshit and hypocrisy in this world drive Queen bananas so she rails against it by writing sons like 'Drop a Deuce.'"

I made a face. "From the sound of it, I would say that just about everything in life drives Queen bananas."

Adnan nodded. "And that's what makes Swarm such a great band."

I sighed. Swarm's music still made no sense; to me, it was just an ear-splitting racket. But the simple fact that Adnan and others found some profundity in it made me feel that perhaps Queen Bea, my bio-mama, was something more than just a screaming, shrieking blonde bitch.

Spurl, that tsunami sometimes raging in my body, was an actual person, just like me. In all the time I had shared my blood and bones with her, I had never considered her human.

CHAPTER 7

May had arrived, finally. High school essentially was a done deal. The instructors had submitted our final grades; all we had to do was show up and hang out. Actually, we didn't even have to show up, but some of us did anyway, and we got into some very enjoyable bull sessions.

What so many of us talked about then was who got lucky enough to be accepted at the colleges worth attending. Adnan had just received his acceptance letter from USC and a half-dozen schools were after Culver even though the little bugger had only decent grades and average SAT scores.

Wizard—surprise!—was heading off to MIT; Ling and Sam Raney had been accepted at Princeton. I still had feelings for Sam and resented him for hooking up with Ling, so I decided it was for the best that the two of them would go back east together and maybe forever.

At home, I had received plenty of mail from Stanford—dormitory assignments and preregistration materials. Even one sorority that apparently wanted me as one of its sisters. The tuition bill was there, and when I opened it and saw the dollar signs, I wondered if I was going to college or buying a mansion. The only reason my dream of attending Stanford had become a reality was the Johnson Scholarship. It would cover the overwhelming majority of my expenses.

Predictably, another innocuous-looking letter, this one from the Johnson Foundation, sat in the pile, and I popped it open with indifference.

Then my heart stopped.

"Dear Ms. Slanz," it started, "we regret to inform you that due to your recent 'cheating' incident during a test-taking event, we must revoke your scholarship," blah, blah, blah.

What are the words to describe my feelings? Devastation, shock, panic, hopelessness. Confusion, too. Not for a moment did I think that my little mishap in the cafeteria with Culver would mean the end of my Johnson Scholarship. Also, the end of my scholarship meant the end of my Stanford education—before it had even started! If Stanford didn't give a rat's ass about what happened that day in the caf, why should the Johnson Foundation?

I had worked part time and saved my paychecks with admirable frugality. Still, my bank balance would scarcely cover the costs of four years at Catatonic State. My freshman year at Stanford would cost nearly fifty thousand dollars! If my infraction in the cafeteria was a big deal, imagine what sort of crime I would have to commit in order to get fifty Ks! I was out of luck so far as Stanford went.

Fuck, I thought. Just fuck.

My parents, too, were heartbroken.

"You'll need forty thousand for Stanford, Christine?" my dad asked with false cheer. "We'll get it somehow. Stanford is worth it. We'll find a way."

"Nix," I said, shaking my head. "That amount of

money is way beyond our means. That's why I applied to some state schools, too—in case that Johnson money didn't happen."

Mom let out a huge sigh. "But you've already notified the state schools that you won't be attending. So I guess you don't have that option left."

"You guess right," I said.

Dad scratched his head. "They withdrew the scholarship because they think you cheated on a test. You didn't cheat…did you?"

"No! Absolutely not! I was tutoring a kid in history because he kept getting dates and places confused. So when it came exam time and he got stuck, I just mouthed a word to him and then one of the teachers busted me for it."

"But why did you even *mouth* anything?" Mom asked. "You know how uptight those people are when it looks like anyone is cheating."

"Look," I told them. "The principal Mr. Schloss? He wanted to punish Chris Culver for being gay. Schloss was, like, 'If you blame this cheating thing on Culver, I'll go along with it.' But I refused."

Mom said, her eyes wide, "Chris Culver? But I thought you didn't like him!"

"I don't have much use for Culver, but I hate Schloss. He wanted me to give him an excuse to expel Culver from school, but I wouldn't go for it."

My folks did their best for me. My mom phoned the school and spoke to Schloss. My dad called the Johnson Foundation. Then they traded places. They spoke loudly and shook their fists.

It was all for nix. The Johnson Foundation would withhold its scholarship and I was going to throw a dozen temper tantrums over my loss.

Dammit!

In retrospect, I probably could have gone to the newspaper and told them all about Schloss and what a bastard he was. But what good would that have done? It definitely wouldn't have gotten me my scholarship back. Of course, to be honest about it, I *was* in the wrong that day in the cafeteria. I *did* cheat—the only difference between me and a million other cheaters was that I got caught.

Dad held his head in his hands. "This whole mess is my fault. If I had stayed in the financial district, pulling down that big money, I could have sent you to Stanford even without that scholarship."

"No, Dad," I replied. "You quit your finance job after Adnan's dad dropped dead right in front of you. You were afraid you'd be next, so you made that huge change of life of leaving finance and buying that corner store. You can't blame yourself for anything. You made the right choice, even if your paydays are smaller."

Adnan's father's fatal heart attack upset me so much that from then on I couldn't say no to him whenever he hit me up for a favor, which was often. I don't think my father believed much of what I had just said to him, and neither did I. He was right; if he'd stayed in that financial district highrise, we would have had the money for Stanford and that Johnson Scholarship would have been unnecessary.

I made a decision: I would keep mum about my non-attendance at Stanford that fall. I could tolerate neither the myriad questions people would ask nor their poor-baby pouts. Naturally, people would start to wonder when September began and I was still doing my summer gig at my father's corner store.

Well, they weren't going to get any explanations from this chick.

"Christine!" Adnan exclaimed. "You'll never guess who's going to be headlining *Punk Off!*"

"Punk *what?*"

He snarled. "Don't be so lame, Christine. *Punk Off!* is *the* touring punk festival. They do it every year, and each one is better than the one before."

"Anyway, this year Swarm is reuniting just for the festival! All the original band members more or less still have their shit together and have agreed to do this."

"Is that good?"

He rolled his eyes. "That's like asking, 'Gee, Adnan, the Beatles are getting back together. Is that good?' Or, 'I understand Jesus is coming back soon. Is that good?'"

"Oh." I should have been thrilled, or excited, or *something* by the news that my bio-mama, after years of reclusion, had agreed to perform with her old band. I had a hard time thinking of her as someone who lived here and now; to me, she was this person from the 1980s who had gained fame and money she didn't deserve and kept doing her thing till she got sick of it and retired. During that time, she had boffed with some dude named Mark Ignas, had me with him and turned me over to the Slanzes.

Anyway, Beatrix Spurl wasn't my mom. Not my real one, anyway. My real one, Missus Slanz, was the lady who got on the phone to the Johnson Foundation and begged them not to do me like that. Their efforts came to nix, but I felt damned grateful that they tried to help.

"Adnan," I said, "why are you impression that I

care about Swarm's reunion?"

He swallowed hard and looked at the ground.

"Furthermore," I told him, "I think Swarm blows lunch. In fact, I have no use for punk music in general. It's not music, it's just shit." An unkind thing to say, certainly, but I enjoyed saying it.

Adnan wouldn't take that sort of crap from anyone else. I had seen him punch out jocks who'd ragged on him about his black clothes. So when I said that unkind stuff to Adnan about punk rock, he gave me a little punch on the arm, which I expected, and which stung a lot. It stung him a lot, too, that I would say such a thing about his beloved punk rock. He expected that kind of talk from the doofuses who were on the sports teams, but not from his oldest friend.

I wish I'd had the guts to offend him a few months earlier by saying something like, "Fuck you, Adnan! I will *not* tutor your friend Culver in history, so don't ask me again. Understand?" If I had said that, I would still have had that Johnson Scholarship and would be going to Stanford in September.

That weekend, Chris Culver came by to see me early in the morning. I don't know if he had the really high IQ some people claimed, but he was supremely gifted at getting on people's nerves.

"What you want? How come you're up? Go away."

He rubbed his eyes. "I've been up all night. Adnan and I waited in line for eight hours to get passes for the *Punk Off!* press conference."

"Nice for you. Did you come all the way over here

to give me the great news?"

He pushed past me and plopped into a big, cushy living-room chair. "Adnan was going to get you a pass, too."

"Well, I'm glad he thought better of it. I've got better things to do than sit in a big room and watch a bunch of star-struck reporters kiss Swarm's asses."

Culver said, "How could you diss punk to Adnan's face like that? It really offended him. You take for granted the friend you have in him."

"Well, if he was such a friend, why did he lean on me to tutor you? I thought you were a pretty ungrateful recipient of my services."

Culver ignored this. "When people laugh at your Young Libs bullshit, Adnan sticks up for you. When people get sick of hearing you run your mouth about Stanford and your Johnson Scholarship, Adnan says it's OK for you to brag because you've earned the right to brag. When people make fun of your nose—"

"Who makes fun of my nose? Nobody does that."

He cackled. "Oh, just everybody. But you should hear Adnan: 'Leave her alone. Christine's a good kid. We've been friends forever. She just gets carried away sometimes.'"

"'She just gets carried away sometimes.' Is that supposed to make me feel better?"

"You should apologize to him."

I had already made up my mind to do exactly that, but was damned if I would give Culver the satisfaction of telling him so.

What I did tell him was, "Culver, piss off."

He nodded. "I said, 'Adnan, don't get Christine a pass,' but he got you one anyway. You're going with us to that press conference."

I shook my head. "Nix to that. I have better things to do than watch a bunch of middle-aged women pretend that they're punks again. They made their bucks, they got old and bored, so they've put on their leathers again and spiked their hair. Swarm is reuniting because of the money and attention they're getting. Leave me out of it."

Culver laughed. "They sure as hell don't need the money. They sold something like twenty-five million CDs and they're always near the top of the list of iTunes downloads.

"For real?" I swallowed hard and pictured the front doors of Stanford swinging wide open for me. My bio-mama, Beatrix Spurl, professionally known as Queen Bea, was rolling in money. I could approach her for the cash to pay my Stanford bills, and if she balked, I could demand it from her. I knew for an absolute fact that I was her kid, so I assumed I had every legal right to insist that she put me through Stanford.

I suddenly had a solution to my big problem, and her name was Queen Bea.

Awesome!

CHAPTER 8

I sat on the downtown-bound train with Adnan and Culver, my mind whirring with the best way of broaching the subject of financing my Stanford education to Queen Bea. Another matter was speaking personally and privately to her, which I supposed was going to be a *very* difficult thing to do.

I had apologized to Adnan, and he forgave me by giving me a big, long hug. I wasn't altogether sure that I deserved his forgiveness. We'd had dozens of conflicts and disputes over the years, but our beefs had little substance, and neither of us could stay angry at the other for very long. Maybe Adnan wasn't as much a tough-guy, hardass punk as we thought. Or maybe he was just so thrilled about Swarm's reunion that even *I* couldn't piss him off.

He sat on the train, smiling. Adnan had such a sweet, friendly smile, I wished he would smile more and scowl less. "It's just unreal," he said as the train rocked us back and forth. "When we get to the hotel, Swarm will be there behind the mics. After all these years! What will they look like in person? Will Queen still be hot? She's given me a boner for all these years."

"Why don't you *not* tell me about it," I said.

Culver said, "I'm sure Queen still looks good.

That's why they're making such a big deal of this reunion. Personally, in my wet dreams, Joey Ramone is *my* main squeeze."

Adnan shrugged. "Whatever turns you on. I think Queen is the hottest woman in punk, which I guess isn't saying much. The thing in punk is to look ugly. The only other sexy woman in punk is Penelope Houston of the Avengers. She still looks terrific. Pretty fuckin' face. Nice ass, too."

"Ho hum." I shifted in my seat as Adnan and Culver leered like kids checking out a nudie magazine. They were going to the hotel to take a look at punk legend Queen Bea, while I was going there to figure out how I would get a private audience with her so I could hit her up for heavy money.

A few months back, I thought that being accepted at Stanford and receiving a Johnson Scholarship were difficult, unsettling tasks. Shit, that was nothing compared to what I was up to right now.

As our train got closer to our stop, Adnan and Culver wouldn't shut up, and I sank lower in my seat. I felt like a sales rep whose future depended upon the call I was about to make, and the product I was about to pitch—myself—was something I doubted my customer wanted and the price I was demanding— enough for a Stanford degree—was far, far too high.

Adnan touched my arm. "Christine, are you all right? This is, like, the greatest day of my life. You should be happy for me."

Culver pointed at me. "She's such a party pooper!"

When we departed the train and finally reached the hotel's ballroom, I nearly wept. Close to a thousand people were already there, sitting butt to butt. The section of the room closest to the action had a sign reading FOR MEDIA ONLY. We struggled to the back of the room, past teenaged punks like Adnan and smartly dressed, graying folks who had slam-danced into each other when Swarm ruled the punk universe a few decades earlier.

We were a zillion miles from where the band would sit. How, I asked myself, will I be able to get a few minutes alone with Queen Bea and state my business?

The answer was: I wouldn't be able to get a few minutes alone with her. She was a celebrity and I was a nobody. In our culture, celebrities keep their distance from nobodies like me.

I was a fool to worry. Adnan, winking at us both, grabbed our hands, and the three of us inched our way past countless people as the interviews began. He'd gotten us right up to the velvet rope that separated the somebodies from the rest of us.

Nearly a dozen bands comprised the *Punk Off!* tour, including Colostomy and Felony, two of the groups, according to Adnan, that were nearly as great as Swarm.

Queen Bea and her girls, naturally, were scheduled to appear last. So the three of us had to listen to all of the others first, mostly a bunch of insipid, uncouth lunks who spat and swore as if they were the Sex Pistols and this was 1978. After a while I couldn't remember which band had said what, and I couldn't have cared less, either.

The audience had its favorites, though. Some of the folks cheered and whistled at Less than Human or Bleeding Ulcers as if seeing old friends after a long separation. The bassist for PTSD had just gotten out of jail after being arrested for beating up on his girlfriend, so the reporters had a few questions for him about that. Still, the main event was the reappearance of Swarm, particularly Queen Bea.

We just had to stay there and wait. After a few hours, they had an intermission and each of us received a lukewarm bottle of water and a bagful of SWAG to admire—a large T-shirt (too small for Adnan), a snapback cap, bumper sticker, ballpoint pen (I wasn't sure how many punks knew how to write) and pocket-sized comb. The tour's logo was a guy with spiky hair and dark glasses sticking his middle finger up his nose. Classy, I thought. Just too damned classy.

By the time the emcee sat back down at his mic to continue with the fun, we'd all been there for what seemed forever; we were sweaty and irritable. So he gave us what we'd come to see.

Swarm.

I would have thought Jesus had bounded onto the stage. The loudest noises came from those aging coots at the back, who shrieked and screamed and carried on as if, well, they were witnessing the Second Coming.

After the procession of leather-clad, aging dipshits acting like latter-day Johnny Rottens and Sid Viciouses, Swarm—the bitchiest, freakiest band in punk history—entered the room one at a time to a deafening ovation. They could have been the mothers, or at least cool aunties, of the hipsters who hung out at every Starbucks I knew. These four women, in leather jackets and easy-fit denims and motorcycle boots, looked to me like four suburban office managers on Halloween, gotten up in their old gear, blushing and bristling at the gales of laughter they expected to hear at work.

Maxie Padz the band's drummer, wore her hair in a smart, short, dark do and had little makeup on. I recognized her from the old images I had seen online; the meanest-looking of the four, she now had a softened, almost harmless-looking countenance. Kitty Litter, who played the bass, had a roundness in her youth that made me assume she'd go to fat as she got older. But no; Kitty looked svelte, even bony. She had a tired look around her eyes—I would have taken her for a Hells Angel's old lady in her biker getup. Rings 'n' Things, known for her jewelry, now wore little or none of it. She looked to me like just another cute, kindly middle-aged broad.

Then I checked out the fourth member of Swarm. The leader of the pack—the mother of modern punk and the woman who had given life to me. I had just spent a few hours enduring punk-rock idiocy and a long, uncomfortable train ride, juggling a dozen mental balls about how to separate Queen Bea from some of her bucks. Yet the moment I saw her—and I don't think she noticed me even for a moment—I felt the strangest kind of serenity.

Behold, I said to myself, this is Spurl. The one on my birth certificate. The ones whose blood flowed through my veins. My presence at the velvet rope, staring at the woman who was such a huge, yet mysterious part of Christine Slanz, somehow trivialized my Stanford plight. I had finally met my biological mother, sort of, and it fascinated me that she and I shared this very special common bond, although I looked nothing like her. Unfortunately.

Adnan threw arm around me. "Look at them! They've still got it!"

I just nodded. I loved seeing Adnan happy.

Queen Bea looked the best—tall, with narrow hips and small breasts. Her shoulder-length blonde hair didn't look like a bleach job. But something was gone from her, and it took me only a few moments to figure it out. Her rage, the unalloyed outrage with which she stalked the stage and scowled at the camera, had been softened into middle-aged complacency. Her Lowness, Queen Bea, the Blonde Bitch of Punk, had sold out and retreated into suburbia with her millions. Now she was back, but perhaps only because she knew that more money awaited her.

Swarm's ovation lasted for ten minutes or more. We applauded; the reporters joined in; the other bands came out to cheer. From all that adulation, one would have guessed that Swarm had cured AIDS, not simply recorded "I Wanna Have Your Abortion."

Once everyone had screamed himself hoarse and gotten sore hands from clapping, Maxie Padz spoke first. "Don't worry," she said. "This time we're going to let you go home."

The crowd roared again, then grew quiet as Swarm answered the many questions the reporters had come to ask.

"Queen, what have you been doing for the past umpteen years?"

She shrugged. "Oh, the usual: Hangin' out, havin' a good time, stayin' stoned and gettin' laid."

Oh, great, I thought. She's gonna be a smartass.

"Bea, what's the best part of being back with Swarm?"

"Being asked intelligent questions by charming people like you."

"Kitty, how have you maintained your guitar skills over the years?"

"I have no guitar skills. I've never had a lesson. I just strum the thing and hope it sounds good. If it sounds bad, I strum it louder."

They all offered up terse, flippant answers, and everyone seemed to eat it up. I figured out that this press conference was just a media event to let Swarm prove that they were still 1985 punks at heart.

"Queen, do you still have your Harley?"

"Yeah, and I use it a lot to run over idiots like you."

Ho hum. Then, the press conference got just a little bit serious. Someone asked, "Queen, all these other gals have families. Do you? If not, what's the deal?"

Queen leaned forward a bit and flashed her ice-blue eyes on him. "It's just the three of us—me, myself and I."

As stupefied by exhaustion as I was, I couldn't stay quiet after hearing *that.*

"No!" I shouted. "That's a lie!"

Adnan grabbed my arm. "Christine—"

I hopped over the rope and pushed past some of the reporters.

"Get back behind the ropes," one of them said. "This is for media only."

I shot him a little snarl. This event had already run on for too long and I felt sure they would wrap it up soon. If I didn't speak to Queen Bea now, I might never have another chance. I hurried forward, knocking aside everyone in my way, scarcely hearing the shouting and yelling directed at me, and stepped over the last rope separating the band.

"Queen, you have a kid! I'm your daughter!"

I reached into my knapsack and pulled out a sealed envelope which contained a copy of my adoption record plus a letter explaining my desire to have her acknowledge our relationship. I stood a dozen feet from Swarm as a couple of burly dudes in black T-shirts closed in on me. I yelled, "Queen, read this!" as I waved the letter at her. She crossed her arms and stared at me.

One of the security guys put his shoulder on my hand and spun me around as if I were a toy. I pushed him off, waved the letter again at Queen and flung it in her direction. My missive nearly hit Kitty Litter in the chin, but she batted it away at the last moment.

"Read it, Queen!" I screamed. "You gotta see it!"

The security guys each got a grip on me and took me away, through one corridor and down another. They opened a big, creaking door and shoved me out. Instantly I smelled garbage and figured out I was in the York's back alley. After looking this way and that, I concluded that the alley let out onto the street to my left, so I went that way and, half a block later, saw the unmistakable York marquee and a huge crowd surrounding the hotel's front entrance.

"Hey!" some kid yelled, gesturing at me. "There's the crazy chick who went after Queen Bea!"

I shook my head and swallowed hard. I realized that these people loitering outside the hotel had come to see Swarm and the other punk bands. The event was now over but the fans hadn't yet dispersed. They had lingered, I observed now, because Swarm's limousine was still parked in front of the main doors. All I saw of the band was Kitty Litter's small, tight butt as she climbed into the car.

I took one last shot. *"Queen! I'm serious! Read the letter! This is no joke!!"*

The door shut with a gentle *chunk* and the big limo eased away.

Some old guy made a face at me. He said, in a mocking voice, "Queen! I'm your kid! You gotta believe me." He shook his head. "I should try that myself on her. 'Queen, I'm your long-lost uncle! Please remember me at Christmas and in your will!'"

Just then the limo's tinted glass slid partway down and I saw Queen. She sat surrounded by the other ladies and she now had on black sunglasses. She looked at me, or at least in my direction, and I couldn't begin to imagine what, if anything, she was thinking.

I called out, "Miz Spurl, I need to talk to you…"

But then the car gained speed, and the people surrounding it jumped away, and soon it was gone.

I burst into tears then and thought—hoped—that the sun would never shine again.

Maybe an hour later, I quit my blubbering and went to get the train for home. I had lost Adnan and Culver. No matter; I wanted to see them as little as they wanted to see me.

After wandering around for a little while, I made it to the train station and boarded the next arrival. I walked through one car, then the next.

Adnan and Culver were there. I plopped down across from them and said, "Hey."

"Piss off," Adnan said. "Don't speak to me."

"You're mad at me over what I did at that press conference."

"Duh." Then, "If you hate the music that I love, that's your problem. But you didn't have to make a fool of yourself in front of Swarm and the rest of the world."

"My bad."

"Music is a huge part of my life, Christine. Swarm means as much to me as Stanford means to you."

"Well, Swarm means a lot more to me than it used to. I seem to have a special relationship with its lead singer. We're sort of like family. Didn't you hear what I said in there?"

"Yes, I heard—and so did many other people." He frowned. "Claiming that someone is your biological parent is a serious matter, you know. Plus, blurting it out at a press conference is a very inappropriate way of going about it."

"I wasn't just claiming that she's my birth mother. I have official papers to prove it."

"Oh? Is that what was in the envelope you threw at them? You almost hit Kitty in the face with it."

"Queen Bea is my mother," I said.

"Then who's that nice lady who lives at your house?"

"She's my adoptive mother. She and my adoptive father got me when Queen decided that having a kid might cramp her style."

Adnan smirked. "Do you expect anyone to believe that?"

"Well, why would I lie about something like this? I'm trying to connect with my birth mother because I think it's the right thing to do."

"Plus, you need money for Stanford, and she's got tons of the stuff." He blew out a sigh, got up and left the car. Culver stayed put.

"How come you didn't leave with him?" I asked.

"I believe what you said about Queen Bea."

"Why?"

"Because," he said, "you look like her."

"I wish."

"No, really. Adnan believes you're Queen's daughter, too."

"Oh, does he?"

"He's mad at you now, but he'll get over it in a few days."

Of course, Culver had said that Ling Chan needed to connect with her inner lesbian, so what did he know?

Culver did have a point about how Adnan's anger would last only a short while. We would be buddies again soon enough. What completely trashed this day was my unsuccessful attempt at introducing myself to Queen Bea and the knowledge that I would have to face a future that excluded Stanford University. Where could I go? What could I do? Well, I didn't have to answer those huge questions in one single day, but when I did get around to finding those answers, I felt pretty sure that I would hate them.

Culver and I did a nice big shut up for the rest of the trip. I even nodded off once or twice. I dreamed of nothing in particular.

When, at last, I traipsed up to our front door, Dad stood there waiting for me.

"Christine," he said, "you were on TV tonight. The six-o'clock news."

"I guess now I'm going to get my fifteen minutes of fame, like Andy Warhol said."

As we went inside, he said, "You look thirsty. Let's get something to drink." He popped open a couple of cans of Sprite and we sipped for a few moments. "Your TV appearance wasn't that long. Just some footage of you rushing through the crowd towards the band, as if you were some kind of Christian fundamentalist with a gun and you wanted to blow them away. They wanted to show that after all these years, Swarm could still make people hate them."

"I didn't go there to blow them away," I said.

"Why *did* you go there? Was it because you wanted to see your mother?"

I pointed past him, to the living room where Mom sat doing a crossword puzzle. "*She's* my mom. *You're* my dad."

He frowned. "So…why did you go there?"

I closed my eyes. "Because I lost my Johnson Scholarship."

"I know."

"But I figured that since I now had a rich relative named Beatrix Spurl, I should go down there and say, like, 'Hey! I need money for Stanford. Give it up.'"

I kept my eyes closed. I hear Dad groan.

"Well," I added, "I would say that I am now completely out of options."

CHAPTER 9

Ling called me during the last week of school to tell me that they had voted me out of the Young Libertarians.

"You're going to be a college woman soon," I said. "Don't you have anything better to do than hassle me?"

Wizard had already given the news, so I already knew about being kicked out of the club. She had even offered to quit as a courtesy to me, but I said no. Wizard loved the Young Libertarians, and they loved her.

Ling said, "Don't take this personally, Christine. It's all about that alleged cheating incident in the caf. I know you lost your Johnson Scholarship because of it, so you sort of look really guilty in that matter. We can't have known cheaters in the club."

"Too bad for me, girlfriend. Guess the club and I will just have to live without each other for these last few days of school."

"Also, you can't use the club as a resume item or as a reference in later life."

"Not a problem," I said. "What we do in high school doesn't mean that much in later life. You could be the Big Man or Big Woman on Campus in high school, but once you're out of there, the world sort of hits the reset button."

I made fun of my predicament, but it really did hurt that I had lost my scholarship and membership in the Young Libertarians. A few months later, in the fall, Ling would be back east at Princeton, with a handsome boyfriend and many glorious things to look forward to in life. And where would I be? I would be minding my father's grocery store, hoping no one would come in and say, "Why, Christine, you're still here! Why aren't you at Stanford? They accepted you, didn't they?"

Soon Ling and I hung up. Two minutes later, the phone rang again.

"Is Christine Slanz available?" The man had a New York accent and a deep voice. At first, I thought he was Larry King.

"My name is Amnon Lichtmann. I'm an attorney," he said. "One of my clients is Queen Bea."

Oh, so my letter *didn't* end up in the shitcan!

"Miz Slanz," he continued, "you need to understand that this whole matter—her status as your birth mother—is a piece of business she thought she had settled years ago."

"Mother-daughter relationships are forever," I told him.

"Not if either party wishes otherwise." Then, "Why have you chosen to contact Queen Bea after all these years? What is the purpose?"

Translation: What do you want from her? Money? Is that what you're after?

Well, yes. But he didn't need to know that just yet. Anyway, I wasn't as greedy as all that—I didn't want to shake her down for millions, or even for a monthly check for the rest of my life. In fact, I would even accept a loan from her; it would have to be enough to cover my costs at Stanford, but Dad and I would figure out some way of paying her back. I just absolutely, positively did not want to surrender my dream of going to that wonderful college.

But again, I didn't need to tell this lawyer any of that just now.

"I want to meet her," I said. "We have something very special in common. I think we should get to know one another."

He must have believed me, because he said, "Are you available to meet with us tomorrow afternoon at two?"

"O.K."

Click.

So, the next day I went back to that big, famous, fancy hotel from which the security boys had given me the bum's rush the day before. But this time nobody hassled me as I took the elevator up to the twentieth floor. I stepped into a huge suite that the *Punk Off!* folks had converted into their business offices. Young men and women in black festival T-shirts and jeans yakked away on cell phones. Band members lay sprawled on sofas, answering reporters' questions.

A cute blonde chick, presumably the receptionist, sat a desk by the front doors and yakked away on the telephone. I stood there like an imbecile for ten minutes, waiting to be acknowledged and told where to go and what to do.

"I'm here to see Amnon Lichtmann," I told her finally.

"Where's Amnon?" she called out.

"He's split," said a ponytailed man at the other end of the room.

I choked back a sob. "But we had an appointment for two this afternoon!"

"Hard luck," said the receptionist.

"But we had some *stuff* we needed to talk about," I said in a thin, dreamy voice. "I wrote a letter and took it with me to that thing downstairs yesterday…"

The guy in the ponytail came up to me. "Oh, you're the kid with the letter. Hope the security guys didn't rough you up too badly."

"No, I survived.

He stuck out his hand. "I'm Finn, Swarm's manager. I'm also Queen Bea's cousin."

We left the main suite headed down a hallway lined with rooms. "Go in," he said.

I did. In that room was a huge leather sofa upon which sat a young woman holding a small voice recorder. The other woman was Queen Bea.

I swallowed hard and stepped backwards. Finn pushed me a bit forward. Queen Bea stood up.

"Shoo," she said, pointing at the woman. The young reporter had now gotten all she was going to get, so she got up and hurried out of the room. Finn left, too. So there I stood, face to face with the bio-mama I knew not at all.

She checked me out. Didn't say a word, just looked and looked. So I looked back. We did this for maybe two minutes, but it felt like a couple of hours.

Finally she said, "Tell me about your parents."

I cleared my throat. "What do you want to know?"

"Have they been kind to you?"

"Oh, yeah, sure. They're great. I mean the world

to them."

"Good. That's good," she said. "So, Christine Slanz, what can I do for you?"

What can I do for you? I didn't know what to say. Actually, I knew many things to say in reply, but none of them would serve my purposes.

Queen Bea was a famous person. Well, so what? She wasn't even famous; she was infamous. Known to vast numbers of people for all the wrong reasons. A Nobel laureate? A negotiator for world peace? Not her; she was beautiful blonde punk-rock bitch who made headlines through her outrageous misbehavior. Her music was dreck, and her notoriety undeserved. It bugged the shit out of me. It really did.

Just then, I cared very little about Stanford or my glorious future. I didn't really even care about the fact that I was in her home, as it were, and that she could have her big boys remove me at any moment. I had some of her nastiness in me, and I took a deep breath as I got ready to run my mouth at her.

But Finn stuck his head inside and said, "Well, is she one of us?"

"Affirmative," replied Queen, tapping her nose.

"Excuse me?" I asked.

"Your nose," said Queen. "It's a genuine Spurl."

I frowned. "I don't get it. Your nose is small and straight. So is his."

She smiled. "That's because we've had ours fixed."

"Why?" I asked.

"Have you ever heard the expression, 'Rock is cock'?"

"Who hasn't?"

"Well, it basically means that in my business, sex appeal matters. Rock fans are funny that way."

"I see."

"About my status as your, uh, relative…we'll get a blood test, just to make it official. The lawyers insist on things like that."

I shrugged. "Whatever."

"The test results," she said, "will take a little while. In the meantime, I think we should get to know each other."

I wasn't sure how we were going to do that. Swarm was going to be on the road, here and overseas, for the next several months. Get to know each other? What would we do, send a zillion tweets every day?

I stayed cool. Meeting Queen Bea had been a disappointing experience—her heart was as cold as the dark side of the moon—but she made my trip to the hotel worthwhile simply by acknowledging, even if she did not wish to do so, that I was Princess Bea. I was hers and she, mine.

The test results would confirm that I had some sort of right to say, "Queen—Mom—I need help with my Stanford tuition…" From a legal standpoint, could she refuse to write me a few big checks?

"Sounds good," I said. "When you get back from your tour, you can pencil me in for a nice long lunch. We can get acquainted then."

She shook her head. "No. One long lunch isn't good enough."

"What, then? You'll be on the road. You don't live here. You're probably the busiest person I know. Where *do* you live, anyway?"

"In Beverly Hills. That's where I have all my stuff. Truth is, I live wherever I hang my hat." Then, "What I have in mind is, why don't you go on tour with us?"

My jaw dropped open.

"To do what?" I asked.

"Be a roadie for the *Punk Off!* tour."

"But I'm a chick."

"Be a chick roadie."

"I didn't know there was such a thing."

She shrugged. "There is now."

I laughed. "Are you sure this can be arranged?"

"I am Queen Bea. I can move mountains."

"Wow."

To Finn she said, "Christine is going on the road with us. Will you have something for her to do?"

He chuckled. "We always have room for one more. It doesn't pay much and she'll break her back, but it will be a great experience."

Queen Bea reached out, shook my hand and smiled. "Welcome aboard. It'll be weird, and you'll work hard, but you'll have fun."

Then she took out her iPhone, pushed some buttons and essentially pretended I had disappeared. Finn pulled me out of the room.

"Don't be offended by Queen," he told me in the hallway. "She tunes people out as soon as she's done with them. It's nothing personal. She just totally concentrates on the business at hand, then moves on to the next item. You can do that when you're the boss."

I nodded. I also wondered if my gig as her roadie would, as promised, be a great experience and I would have fun. I knew it would be weird.

CHAPTER 10

People were right when they talked about how Queen Bea was like a drug—no matter how much you got of her, it wasn't enough. I must have been stoned without knowing it, because I promised to work for her that summer on the Alienation tour without even consulting my parents on the matter.

I thought about their reaction plenty as I took out my cell phone and called home from outside the hotel.

After the usual hello-and-what's-up, I said, "Dad, before I forget, I won't be able to work for you this summer."

"Oh? Did you get a better deal? Did the Libertarians offer you an internship or something?"

"Not exactly."

"Well, spill it."

I closed my eyes and took s deep breath. "I'm going to be a roadie for Swarm on the Alienation tour."

He guffawed. "You're such a kidder, Christine. Now tell me the truth."

"Just like I said." I told him about my little meeting in the hotel.

There was an awful silence. Then, "Do you know what you're getting into? Do you know what happens during those concert tours?"

"They're not as bad as all that," I said.

"Oh, really? Do you remember when Swarm went on tour? They attracted every lowlife in every city. That Queen Bea told her fans to riot in the streets, so that's what they did."

"Dad, that was many years ago. Things have changed. So has Queen Bea."

"I seriously doubt that."

I blew out a huge breath. "Look, I'm doing this for the bucks so I can go to Stanford. I totally goofed up my scholarship, so this is my only option left."

"Let me see if I understand this matter. Queen Bea is going to pay you forty thousand dollars so you can go to Stanford, and in exchange you're going to work on her crew. Is that about right?"

"I haven't asked her for the money yet. She's ordered tests to confirm that she's my mother. When the tests come in, I'll be in a pretty good position to say, 'You're my birth mother and I need this money for Stanford, so you sort of owe me this.'"

"Hmm."

"Like I said, I've pretty much run out of options."

Another prolonged pause. Then, "I want to meet her. Queen Bea."

"Too late. The tour starts in a few days."

"Listen, if Queen Bea wants to take *my teenaged daughter* on the road for the summer, she's going to have to meet with me in person and say, 'Mister Slanz, I personally guarantee that Christine will be safe and happy throughout the tour.' Otherwise, you're staying home and working for me this summer."

"No chance, Dad. This Swarm reunion thing is a pretty big item. You'd never get in to see her."

"Is she at the Hotel Bayporte? Are you still there?

I'll be there in an hour. Wait for me."

"Dad! Negative—"

Click.

I looked here and there, full of anxiety. I had heard an unnameable something in my father's voice that had been absent for years. The last time I had heard such a tone from him was when his colleague had dropped dead and Dad had given up his high-powered, high-paying finance job. When Rudy Slanz decided he was going to do something, that was that. I couldn't feature him on the seat of a chopper as it crashed through a window, but in his own way, he was just as stubborn and determined as Queen Bea.

The prospect of introducing these two people to each other freaked me out. Queen Bea was a punk goddess; my father was the proprietor of a small, humble corner grocery store. Queen Bea could pull forty thousand dollars out of her butt with no discomfort; Dad had to watch every dime that came in or went out. Queen Bea had bumped uglies with someone named Mark Ignas, had his baby, lost interest in the baby-daddy and baby, and moved on; Rudy Slanz had raised that baby, and now he and I were going into the hotel to visit—confront?—Queen Bea. Would anything good come of this?

At around dinnertime I stood outside the Hotel Bayporte, waiting for my father to arrive. Forty-five minutes later, he emerged from the hotel's parking lot, scowling and pointing in the direction of where he'd left his car.

"Parking in this place is almost as expensive as staying here. I wonder if Queen Bea would validate my ticket."

"We don't have to go up there and bug her."

"Well, we're here, so let's do it."

I shrugged, and we went inside. We took the elevator up, and when we arrived at our destination, we encountered as much disorder as I had experienced earlier. Colostomy had arrived, and its long-haired, leather-clad members made faces and posed for pictures. Bass guitarist Jimmy Hove wore on his left wrist a chunky, gleaming watch that must have been a platinum Rolex. My father rolled his eyes.

"Faker," he muttered.

"What?"

"You see that watch? No *real* punk walks around wearing a Rolex that costs more than a car. Punks are supposed to hate luxury stuff."

"You know about punk values? Punk culture?"

"Punk has been around a long time, kiddo. It's all about rebelling and having contempt for the middle class. The Sex Pistols sort of understood that, but these clowns don't."

"Did Swarm understand what being punk was all about?" I asked.

"They came after the Sex Pistols. But, yeah, I guess they did. All the big punk acts came through here years ago—the Sex Pistols, the Ramones, D.O.A., the Dead Kennedys, Iggy Pop."

"So you know the punk scene."

He shrugged. "I knew it when I was young and angry."

All around us, everyone seemed to make a point of pretending we weren't there. Dad looked around, squared his shoulders and went up to a young lady seated at a desk.

"I want to see Queen Bea," he told her in a very loud voice.

She looked up at him with a smirk as a bald, burly guy came to the desk and said, "You want something with her?"

"I'm the father of Queen's daughter."

The burly guy said, "She's rapping to the press right now. Maybe we can get you in for a few minutes later on. You'll just have to wait."

Dad nodded. "We'll wait."

Together we squeezed onto a leather sofa. People kept coming and going, many of them nasty looking critters in torn jeans and studded-leather jackets. Soon a server pushed in a cart filled with iced champagne bottles. Then someone else wheeled in a hot buffet tray. I took a nice long whiff of the delicious aroma and suddenly realized how hungry I was.

"Looks like they're having a party," I said to Dad.

"I wonder if we're invited."

Just then, Jimmy Hove and some tricked-out party girl plopped down onto the sofa next to us and started getting friendly. Then Queen Bea and her cousin Finn came in from another room, and everyone turned to smile at them. The two of them yawned, as if they were exhausted and wanted to go away.

Queen Bea saw me on the sofa and said, "Hey"— she snapped her fingers—"Christine, right? Back for more? Or have you been sitting there all this time?"

"This is my dad, Queen," I said in a tiny voice. "He wanted to meet you."

My dad got up. "I've come to talk to you, Bea. I know that you're my daughter's birth mother, but her adoptive mother and I have been raising her for quite a while now. So let me give you the benefit of my years of parenting: Before you take a seventeen-year-old girl on a coast-to-coast punk-rock tour with a bunch of people who are very much like yourself, just make sure that the teenaged girl won't see anything she shouldn't see. Exhibit A"—he pointed to Jimmy Hove and the party girl, who were making out on the sofa.

I sat and stared at Queen Bea, who I thought might tell a few of her roadies to hustle us out of the hotel. But no; the punk legend just stood there, frowning. Not offended, just bemused.

Queen Bea put her hands on her narrow hips and asked, "What do you want us to do for her?"

Dad frowned, as if he had been expecting, and perhaps hoping for, a knee to the groin so that he, in retaliation, could grab her by her shoulder-length blonde hair and bitch-slap her till her pretty face was little more than a couple of huge welts.

"What?"

"When Christine goes on tour with us, I'll make it clear that if anyone looks at her the wrong way, they'll have to deal with me personally. Is that what you had in mind?"

Dad nodded. "Yeah. I think so."

"Then it's a deal. Shake." Queen extended her hand, which Dad accepted.

"Cool," she said, then blew out of the room with Finn.

Dad just stood there, scratching his head, perhaps searching for the moment where he would get to tell her off in front of everyone. Instead, Queen had handled him pretty well, and if he had anything to say now, he would be talking to himself.

What he said was, "I think your mother's gonna freak out when we tell her about this."

CHAPTER 11

My mother had always loved to do crossword puzzles—that was her escape from the world. When Dad and I came home, she lay curled up on our sofa with her nose in a puzzle. We told her about our adventure, and she tsked. "Wonderful. My teenaged daughter is going on that weirdo punk tour."

"It's called *Punk Off!*" I said.

"She's nearly of age," Dad said. "It's time we cut her some slack and let her get some real-world experience."

"Did you tell that middle-aged punk slut that we'll sue her to kingdom come if Christine gets victimized in any way?"

Dad nodded. "We had a talk. Queen Bea knows that she needs to look out for Christine when they're on the road."

I heard nothing more from Queen, but Finn emailed me information about the DNA testing, and then the Fed Ex truck came by with a package of details concerning the *Punk Off!* tour.

I was in!

"Christine's effort and dedication have made her one of our most honored and admired students and brought her early acceptance at Stanford." The principal smiled and some of the students even applauded as I stepped up to receive my diploma.

I could have punched him out. After all, Kerr knew about my scholarship and why it had been revoked; he also knew that the closest I'd ever get to Stanford would be a day trip to visit its campus. Plus, that creep actually took credit for my success even though I had done all the work, not him.

As furious as I was, Spurl wanted to kill that creep. The simple fact that I was tour-bound with Swarm scarcely pacified the Spurl cells raging within me. Queen Bea was now my birth mother *and* my boss. I felt more determined than ever to get her to contribute heavily to my Send Christine to Stanford Fund.

I clapped my hand over Spurl's big mouth and bounded off the stage to high fives and handshakes. Suddenly Adnan was right in front of me but not looking at me. I wasn't sure of what to say to him. We hadn't spoken since my little performance at the *Punk Off!* press conference.

"Congrats, Christine." He didn't smile.

"Right back at ya." I nodded at Ewan, who stood alongside Adnan. "You, too, guy." Minutes earlier, Kerr had gone on so effusively about Ewan's accomplishments that it sounded as if the principal had been the kid's mentor or something.

"So," Adnan said, still refusing to make eye contact, "did you contact, you know…"

"Yeah, I know. We sat down and talked. She was cooperative."

Adnan swallowed hard. "Uh, did you work something out?"

"She owned up to it. I'm her kid. We're doing DNA testing just to make sure. But apparently I have the family trait." I tapped my nose.

Adnan frowned. "She doesn't have a big nose."

I smirked. "Not any more."

His jaw dropped. "You mean she got a nose job? For real?"

I nodded. "Can you imagine? Once upon a time, she looked like me!"

I waited for Adnan to say, "Come *on*, Christine! You had a sit-down with Queen Bea? I want to know every word you said to each other." But no; this time he turned away. My relationship with him went back to when we were toddlers. We'd begun life with something close to nothing in common—little girls and boys tend not to like each other at that age, anyway—and with each passing year became even more different. But even as Adnan grew into a black-jacketed nihilist and I into a Levi's-clad libertarian, we were always civil and often friendly to one another. Who could have guessed that the one thing we truly had in common would have driven a wedge between us?

Adnan adored Queen Bea the way most boys fell in love with movie beauties. I could understand why he felt that way; she had shiny platinum hair, perfect features and, when she wasn't scowling, a big blonde smile. If I were a lesbian, I would be horny for her, too. Adnan should have been thrilled to learn that I was Queen's daughter, but instead he seemed to resent me for having a special place in her life.

Ewan said, "Christine, I think it's totally awesome that you're her daughter." Then the dummy added, "After you hit her up for the Stanford bucks, make sure you get her to buy you a rhinoplasty, too."

"Thank you very little," I retorted as I beat cheeks

out of there.

CHAPTER 12

From the way my mom acted at the airport, one would have thought that it was 1968 and they were shipping me off to Vietnam, where I would get killed or become so shell-shocked that they would ship me back home in a straitjacket.

As my MacBook Pro went through the metal detector, my mom cried out, "Christine! Can you ever forgive me?"

"Huh?"

"Can you ever forgive me for being so mean that I've driven you to run off with a traveling freak show?"

I shook my head. "That's not how it is, Mom. This is a good opportunity. Wish me well."

I turned to Dad, and he shrugged, as if he, too, felt my new adventure might be a idea. "You can still back away from this, Christine. You don't have to do it. She can find another roadie."

I wanted to stand there for a few minutes and say some sincere, poignant things to them about how they always had been and always would be my family. But the airport was a busy place, and I had to board my flight. "Gotta go. See ya."

This would be the last time I saw Mom and Dad before being strip-searched. If I had known at the airport that a strip-and-squat might happen to me, I would have turned around and gone back home with my folks. I wasn't about to drop my drawers for nobody.

The vibrations were bad, very bad, as soon as I boarded the aircraft. My tray table was sticky, so the flight attendant had to wipe it down. Then they didn't have Sprite, so I had to settle for 7-Up. We had some turbulence that shook the plane hard enough to make overhead lights go on and off. Our destination was Los Angeles, but we landed in Las Vegas and sat there for a few hours while the mechanics and technicians tried to figure out why our lights had gone on and off. Finally they shrugged, said they didn't know what the problem was, and gave up. The airline had no other aircraft available, so they herded us off the plane, packed us into a bus and drove us to Los Angeles International Airport, six hours away. If anyone from Swarm or *Punk Off!* had gone to the airport to meet me, they had left hours ago. So I did the only logical thing: I got into a taxi and told the driver I needed to go out to the concert site— Highland Park Raceway. "Yeah!" he shouted, pumping his fist as he stowed my suitcases into his trunk. "Get in!"

I didn't know why he felt so overjoyed until he pulled onto the freeway and his meter's numbers flew by so fast that I could scarcely read them. By the time he let me out, the ride cost me just over one hundred ten dollars. As I handed over my debit card and insisted on a receipt, I wondered if Swarm, *Punk Off!* or whoever did the accounting for this music festival, would bitch and moan about reimbursing me for that outrageously expensive taxi ride.

Punk Off! began at noon and ended at around midnight. Swarm, the main attraction, went on last, so its members wouldn't even be at the site when I arrived. But I was a roadie, and we were supposed to be there to set up the equipment for Swarm as soon as Colostomy, the preceding act, finished its set.

I paid the cabbie, mostly unable to hear myself think as the music roared through the southern California evening sky. He popped open his trunk, dumped my suitcases at my feet and sped off. I stood there and looked around—this venue appeared to be in the middle of nowhere, if southern California could be described that way. I knew that attendance at this thing was about fifty thousand, and all of them seemed to be screaming at once.

Someone came up from behind me and tapped me on the shoulder. I turned around and saw a very big dude whose windbreaker had STAFF emblazoned on the front. I showed him my crew badge. He took one of my suitcases, I took the other one and slung my knapsack around my shoulder. As we traipsed along, another man joined us.

"Christine!"

I didn't hear his bellowing voice as much as I read his lips. His name was Rudy; he worked as the chief roadie or something.

Where you been? his lips asked. *You're way late!*

Not my fault, I lipped back. *I'll tell you later.*

He led me to a golf cart where we stored my suitcases and knapsack. Its driver took off and we bulled our way to the edge of the stage.

The time had come for Christine Slanz to get busy and go to work. Colostomy was on stage now; Swarm would be next.

The backstage area seemed insanely crowded, too. Swarm had arrived, and the half-dozen or so other bands stood around with their managers, crew and hangers on. Virtually all of them had already performed. The opening act, Abortion, had finished up hours earlier but stuck around, I supposed, because it was *Punk Off!* and they didn't want to miss anything. The festival's full number of bands, managers and whatnot milled about. So did rock-music reporters and photographers, plus some people I didn't recognize who were important enough to hang out there and not be asked to bugger off. The night's final act, just moments away, would be Swarm's reunion after many years apart. A very big item.

I dodged and weaved around people in my search for Queen Bea. Finally I found her; she stood hidden from view by a stack of amplifiers.

"Queen! I'm so sorry I'm late! My flight ended up in Vegas and they had to bus me in—"

She shot me a look of such indescribable rage that at first I feared she would punch me out. Then she stormed off, and I thought that might be her way of saying, "You're fired!"

Finn must have seen us, because he hurried up to me and shouted a tiny bit above the din, "Damn, Christine, don't mess with her head after she's psyched herself up for a performance! She'll bite off your tongue and spit it back in your face!"

I regarded my birth mother as she surveyed the stage lights, her face still taut, eyes narrowed—and I could have sworn seeing smoke ooze from her ears. I knew enough to recognize her attitude as the Queen

Bea venom she'd injected into her fans from back in the 'Eighties. Today, it remained as much a part of her as those studded-leather stage suits she always wore.

I squared my shoulders and marched up to Finn. I told him of my sticky airline tray, the turbulence, our landing in Las Vegas and my bus ride the rest of the way. I also mentioned my taxi ride that cost over a hundred dollars.

He shrugged. "No big thing, girlfriend. We're all learning as we go along. We're asking ourselves, 'Will it rock or will it suck?' Just do what the other roadies are doing and you'll be fine." Then, "You've brought way too much luggage. You'll learn soon enough that traveling light is the best way to go. For example, most of the bands buy disposable undies. They perform, sweat it through and dump it. Doing laundry is an unnecessary luxury when you're on the road."

I laughed. "If Queen Bea, at the end of her set, pulled off her soaking-wet panties and tossed them into the audience, that would make some souvenir."

"Oh, her audience would fight over her panties and end up pulling them apart."

We both laughed, and I felt grateful to Finn for taking time to explain these facts of life to me just minutes before Swarm went on after a sixteen-year hiatus. My birth mother may have been a frightening, self-obsessed creature, but at least Finn was a decent enough guy.

He handed me a small plastic package and pointed to his ears, into which he had stuffed little foam things—earplugs. I nodded, tore open the package and inserted the plugs into my own ears. I gave him the thumbs up. He mouthed, *Sit on the amplifiers if you want a good view.*

I nodded and climbed up a stack of them. I sat next to a woman music writer from the *L.A. Underground Free Press.* The crowd started stirring, shouting and screaming, seeing that midnight had come and Swarm would appear within a few minutes.

Presently the stage lights dimmed and the audience's cheers made the emcee's words almost inaudible: "Ladies and gentlemen"—no such people existed in *this* crowd—"please welcome Wretched Records recording artists Swarm!"

I cupped my hands over my ears to keep my eardrums from popping out of my head. Tens of thousands of punks shrieked at the same moment that someone plucked a guitar string. Then the other instruments joined in and I thought the whole racket might trigger a major earthquake that would open up the ground and swallow us all.

I didn't like punk music, and knew I never would. But I had to admit that Colostomy, the band I had just heard, sounded like kids goofing around with musical instruments in someone's garage compared to the kind of noise Maxie Padz, Kitty Litter and Rings 'n' Things began making in the southern California desolation.

For the briefest moment I forgot that one of the band's members still hadn't appeared on stage yet. Then, with a flash of stage lighting, Queen Bea appeared and I thought the whole world might end.

I'd downloaded Swarm's music from iTunes and perused images of the band. I saw four young, middle-class white women, punked out and full of attitude, making faces and sticking out their middle fingers. They seemed then to be having lots of fun running a head trip on the straight world.

As Queen Bea scowled and screamed and shrieked, so did all those who had come to see her. I sure couldn't understand the lyrics, but perhaps that was the point: the world, according to Swarm, was a pretty incomprehensible place.

I turned to look at the *Underground* reporter sitting next to me. She had her eyes closed and tears streamed down her cheeks, as if the Second Coming had finally happened. A moment later she wiped her face and watched Queen Bea as if that punk rocker were, indeed, the Messiah.

I did the same thing. I got freaked out by the fact that the woman on stage was someone with whom I shared a large, misshapen nose and many other qualities. Also, as I sat on that stack of amplifiers, I started to think of how many hours I had been up and how exhausted I felt. But who really cared about that? I had made it here after all, to see that part of me I had never understood—the Christine Slanz who had come from Beatrix Spurl. For I knew, and could not deny, that the tall, skinny blonde running from side to side on that stage was the answer to the question, *Who is Christine Slanz?*

I had never met Mark Ignas, and for all I knew he was a conservative, respectable man who had somehow gotten involved with Queen Bea and impregnated her with what turned out to be me. I guess that he, like all other heterosexual men, found her completely irresistible.

Swarm, unlike Colostomy, spent little time verbally abusing their audience, although I could guess that Queen Bea's main spoken message, mostly distorted to my ears, was this: You suck, the world sucks, society sucks, so why haven't you burned it all down yet and replaced it with something new and better? If you're unhappy and your life is awful, get off your lazy butt and make a new world! The crowd cheered and cheered but clearly had no intention of busting out of there and tearing down whatever it was Queen wanted destroyed.

Still and all, Swarm, if one did not eyeball them too closely, looked much as they had years earlier, with their firm boobs, tight bellies and small bums. Their anger, real or not, meant, to me at least, that they were still "the bitchiest band in the land."

The final song of their set, "Nuke 'Em and Smile," according to Adnan, was the band's last recording ever.

Adnan, I thought with a smile as, next to me, the *Underground* music reporter sat and bawled all over her notebook till it became just a soggy wad of nothing. Adnan should be here for this event, I said to myself.

At the end of their last song, Queen Bea tossed aside her microphone and flung herself into the audience (actually they were roadies); Maxie Padz kicked apart her drum kit and threw her sticks into the crowd; and Kitty Litter pulled off the strings of her plugged-in guitar so hard that I felt the feedback from my teeth to my toenails.

Rings 'n' Things began doing a bizarre martial-arts dance, the same one she had done so many years earlier. She leapt high into the air, chopping and kicking, and when she went down with a thud, she just lay there, in the fetal position, for the longest time.

CHAPTER 13

As a roadie, I had the job of making myself useful wherever and whenever necessary, so I rode in the ambulance as it sped towards the hospital.

"Faster!" Rings' face contorted with pain as she lay curled up in the ambulance.

"What happened to you?" asked the paramedic as he knelt by her side.

"I fell down and hurt myself," she replied through gritted teeth.

I said, "What happened was, she did some fancy jumps and kicks and landed the wrong way. Maybe it's her back that's the problem."

"Not my back." Rings started sweating. She swallowed hard. "It's my stuff."

"Your what?" I asked.

She took a deep breath and rolled her eyes. "My junk. My va-ju-ju."

"Oh."

Rings fixed her eyes on me. "Who you? You work for me?"

The paramedic said, "Ma'am, I have to find out what's wrong with you."

She snarled. "Just get me to a damn hospital so they can fix me up."

When we reached the hospital, the doctor checked her out and said, "You're more right than wrong: Hernia that you aggravated by doing those kicks on stage. Need to operate."

"When?" Rings asked.

"Right now."

Rings scowled. "I can't believe I hurt myself by doing those kicks. I used to do them all the time with no problems."

"When was your last kick?" asked the doctor.

"About twenty years ago."

"Well, I could run the four-forty in under a minute twenty years ago, but no longer."

As the orderlies wheeled Rings into the operating room, I took out my iPhone and dialed the only number I had for this festival: Finn's.

"Who is this? I'm very busy!"

"Finn, this is Christine. We have a problem. Rings just went into surgery to have something fixed."

For the next several moments I heard only laughter, music and the clinking of glasses. No Finn.

"Are you there? Did you hear me? I said that Rings is having an operation right now."

"Don't bug me. I'm trying to solve our problem."

"Sounds like there's a party going on."

"There is." He paused. "She's having minor surgery, right? So she'll be able to make our San Francisco gig."

"Negative. She'll need weeks to recover from this."

After swearing many times, he said, "This is the first day of *Punk Off!* and suddenly we have no Rings. I swear to God, I am jinxed."

"Stop feeling sorry for yourself," I told him. "You're not being operated on. It's Rings."

"Yeah, right, whatever. You need to stay there with Rings. I'm sending Rudy over to get you. I would do it myself, but I need to find a replacement for Rings, and they're all here at this party."

I rolled my eyes. "She's in the hospital, and you're at a party."

"You need to understand something. In the music business, parties are actually meeting places. I mean, everyone is eating barbecue and drinking imported beer and it *looks* like a party, but they're really pitching ideas and exchanging business cards. Down by the swimming pool, where it looks like they're just tanning and *schmoozing*, some very heavy deals get done." I heard some female purring, and Finn muttered, "Later, sweetie."

"Is Queen Bea there?" I asked.

"Negative. Make sure you look around for Rudy when he gets to the hospital. He'll be there soon. And thanks for being there for Rings, girlfriend."

I seemed to be about the only person who gave a crap about her. I wished Finn would stop calling me "girlfriend."

Despite Finn's promise to send Rudy over to help me deal with Rings, nobody showed up, so I hung out near the OR. I waved hi at unconscious Rings as they rolled her out of surgery at something like three in the morning. By dawn, I had curled up in a plastic chair in the ER waiting room and dozed off. Funny how easily sleep came when I'd been up for close to twenty-four hours.

I was in the middle of an erotic dream starring some cute guy when I felt myself being shaken awake.

"Wakey, wakey, sleeping beauty!"

I looked up. "Rudy. So glad you could make it." I sniffed. "You've been drinking all night."

"But of course." He swallowed a tiny alcoholic

laugh.

He escorted me out of the waiting room and into the parking lot, to a van full of loud roadies and chicks.

"You're all drunk," I said. "I'll drive."

"Yes, ma'am!" Rudy shouted into the sunrise as he handed me the keys to the dusty Ford van.

We cruised around for the longest time, mainly because none of them could quite remember where the Hyatt was. We stopped for gas and to ask directions, and that's when the chicks said they needed to use the ladies' room. On their way, they got a better offer from some other guys and took off.

By and by we found the Hyatt. I traipsed up to my room, which turned out to be a double. "Hey, roomie," said Rudy as he traipsed along with me.

"I'm not sharing a room with you."

He shrugged. "Got no choice. The hotel is all booked up. But don't worry—I think I can manage to keep my hands to myself."

Rudy invited the other guys to come in for a little while. "Don't worry about them either, girlfriend. I think they'll manage to keep their hands to themselves, too."

"Well," I said, "I'm dead tired, so I'm going to get some sleep."

So the other guys came in and behaved like Neanderthals. They raided the minibar and told dirty jokes that totally grossed me out. I tried to pretend I was sleeping, but then Rudy said they should all shake up some cans of Coors and spray each other with foam, just for fun. I knew *I* would end up drenched, so I sat up in bed and said, "Rudy, if you guys get one drop of that stuff on me, I will kick your balls up through the roof of your mouth!"

Rudy and his boys stared at me for a moment. A tall, skinny, big-nosed chick with messy, frizzy blonde hair, I probably did not seem like someone who should be taken seriously.

Then we heard a knock on the door.

"Get lost!" yelled Rudy.

"Christine?"

Rudy gulped. He jumped over to the door and threw it open. "Queen! Sorry! Didn't know it was you!"

I waved and beamed as she entered the room. Rudy and his doofus friends scrambled to get out of her way as she headed towards me. "Christine, you really look like hell."

"Thank you very little," I retorted. "I've been awake, like, forever."

"Then maybe you should get some sleep."

"Damn straight." I added, "Finn sent me in the ambulance to the hospital to keep Rings company. She hurt herself on stage, you know. She can't do the rest of the tour."

Queen shrugged, as if I had just told her that Rings had a hangnail. "I came by to see if you wanted to grab some breakfast," she said to me. "But it looks like you need some sleep instead." She turned around and headed for the door. Then she spun and said, "I'm sure Rudy and these boys will stay nice and quiet so you can sleep."

Rudy and his boys looked from me to her, all of them nodding and looking down at the floor and.

"Sorry we couldn't get you a private room or at least one with another chick," Queen Bea said. "But you're my girl, so if anyone mistreats you, they'll have my boot up their butt."

Then she left the room. Rudy wheeled around to me. "What was that all about? Are you related to Queen Bea or something?"

I didn't reply, I just lay back down, rested my head on the fluffy, fresh-smelling hotel pillow and went to sleep for the longest time.

CHAPTER 14

The rest of the roadies drove up to their next gig in the equipment trucks—which, I supposed, made sense since they were called roadies. I, however, flew up with Queen Bea and the rest of Swarm. "You can use Rings' ticket," she explained. "We can hang out together for an hour or so and visit."

Well, we flew up together, but we didn't have much of a visit. Queen was a fool to think she and I would just get to hang out and chat, seeing as how she *was* Queen Bea, as in Swarm, and this was their first time together in many years, and—most important—she still looked gorgeous. Music's best bad girl was back, and the rock world had a few zillion questions to ask her.

She pushed me into a limousine and crawled in behind me. Across from us sat a man who smiled at us. "He's from *Rolling Stone* or something," Queen told me. She'd promised him an interview, and that was the only time she could squeeze him in.

At LAX, Maxie Padz stood by our charter jet. At his feet sat a Saint Bernard on a leash.

"We didn't buy a ticket for no pooch!" Rudy shouted.

"His name's Bernie," said Maxie, "and he's going up with us."

Rudy shook his head and laughed. "A Saint Bernard named Bernie. Gee, how creative."

"Well," she said, "*I'm* stuck with him, so *we're* stuck

with him."

"How did you end up with Fido—"

"Bernie."

"Whatever."

"See, my ex," Maxie told him, "was supposed to look after Bernie, but his secretary said, 'Let's go away for the weekend and chill,' so they did. *Someone* has to look after our big baby, right?"

"Couldn't you find a kennel?" Rudy asked. "I don't like the idea of a big, slobbering Saint Bernard as part of a punk band's entourage. Someone might take his picture and post it online. It would embarrass us."

Maxie threw up her hands. "A kennel? Negative. I don't want *my* dog to get kennel cough—or worse."

"We're not having that big beast on tour with us," said Rudy.

Maxie said, "I am married to this creep who makes much less money than I did, so if we call it quits *he* gets to keep the house that *I* paid for. So we have this kid, right, and she's decided she wants to go to Yale and she expects me to pay for that. I'll end up in bankruptcy court when all this is over with."

Presently some men wheeled a big pet container towards us and Bernie, with some reluctance, crawled inside. They loaded him into the baggage compartment as he cried and moaned.

"The pooch stays in Frisco," said Rudy. "We'll book him into a kennel and get him back once the tour is over."

"Negative," said Maxie as she glowered at him. "You try to pull a stunt like that and I'll quit the tour. Rings is a big question mark right now, and Swarm definitely doesn't need to lose another original member right now." Maxi cupped her hands around her mouth and hollered at the pet container, "Don't cry, baby! Mommy loves you!"

"That dog isn't so bad," Queen Bea whispered into my ear. "Her old man is the real animal."

Soon after we boarded the aircraft and our pilot lifted us above the Los Angeles smog, Rudy stood up.

"OK, sports fans," he said, "here's the deal. Dina Dinner of the Menstrual Cramps has agreed to fill in for Rings. Dina said, 'Swarm's music is so easy that any retard can play it,' which I'm taking as a compliment. Even so, we're going to have a rehearsal with her just to make sure she knows our stuff." He paused and looked past us for a moment. "Rings' accident was unfortunate, but we have to remember that Swarm is now a bunch of middle-aged women, not some kids who can do those fancy kicks without having to worry about personal injuries. You've got to go out there and be Swarm, and do the songs your fans love, but always remember that you're not young anymore." He grinned at me. "Except you."

He turned to Kitty Litter as she sat stuffing doughnuts into her mouth. "Also, let's go easy on the carbs, huh? Our butts don't have to get any bigger than they already are."

Kitty made an obscene finger gesture at him and said, through a mouthful of carbs, "Kiss mine."

"Don't speak when your mouth is full," said Rudy. "Anyway, I'm just looking out for Swarm and what's best for the band."

"Well," Kitty said, swallowing her mouthful of carbs, "I'm famished and these things are yummy."

"If you're famished, snack on fresh fruits and veggies."

"Those things aren't yummy like doughnuts," retorted Kitty.

"And they aren't fattening like doughnuts, either," Rudy said. "Anyway, we have people to meet and questions to answer when we land in the Bay Area. Let's go over that now…"

He went into much detail on a dozen items, and when he finally shut up and sat back down, I finally figured out that my mother-daughter chat with Queen Bea had not happened and probably never would. I shot a quick look at the woman who had given birth to me. She just sat there, her eyes closed, and listened to whatever crap was blaring through her headphones. I was the farthest thing from her mind.

Sign-waving protestors stood outside the entrance of the Jeremy, our San Francisco hotel.

I looked out the window and shuddered. "There must be a couple hundred of them."

Queen Bea chuckled. "This city cracks me up. They always need something to bitch about."

I couldn't read what the signs said but guessed that none said WELCOME SWARM. We stepped out of the limousine and walked past the sneering, shouting mob who might have spat or thrown things at us except for the dozen or so cops who stood a couple of feet away.

I leaned towards Queen Bea and said, "It's weird to have so many people hate you."

"Weird but fun." She turned to the mob and made an especially lewd tongue-flick.

Rudy pointed to a sign reading RINGS IS EVIL. "Evil won't be here today," he yelled at the sign holder. "She has PMS."

Kitty Litter led Bernie by his leash. He stopped directly in front of a cluster of protestors to squat and drop a huge, pungent deuce. Some groaned and stepped away, waving away the big dog's stink.

We hurried into the lobby and nearly fell on top of each other as we roared with laughter. Even Queen Bea sat on the carpet, wiping tears away from her reddened face. Maxie, holding her aching sides, bent double and kissed Bernie on his forehead. Then she pointed at Rudy. "And *you* wanted to stick my baby in some smelly kennel!"

To paraphrase the legendary Bette Davis, being a roadie ain't no job for sissies. We have to assemble and break down equipment weighing hundreds of pounds. Set it up, wait till the show's over, then take it apart, pack it into trucks and haul it off to the next city. So your boss is a major rock star? Big deal; the rock star *schmoozes* with the press; the roadie gets sore muscles, squashed fingers and toes and severe electric shocks. Once, when plugging in someone's guitar, I got a jolt that fried the short-and-curlies between my legs. Chico even swore he could see smoke rising from the waistband of my Levi's.

Punk Off! had its own crew to look after the stage, lighting and speaker towers. The bands themselves had to provide their own people to manage their equipment. For Swarm, I ran around all day in a black T-shirt and jeans, doing myriad things that nobody else wanted to bother with.

The really time-consuming work was the flunky stuff like hustling over to the drugstore for Midol and

Preparation H or picking the green candies out of the jars of M&M's so that Queen Bea wouldn't see them, and putting them back in for Kitty Litter, who said that the green ones tasted the best. I thought that was the weirdest thing I had ever heard.

"Can you read OK?" Kitty asked me.

"I guess."

"Well, *I* can't." She flung a document into my lap. "Print's too small. Tell me what it says." She had me making secret trips to get her burritos and Pabst Blue Ribbon beer even though Rudy insisted that Kitty stay on her diet and remain svelte.

"Nobody likes a fat punk," he'd said many times.

Ironically, the person I connected with the least, Queen Bea, was the one who interested me the most. The other roadies kept escorting her to interviews and four-minute TV appearances, and Chico, who handled such plum assignments, gave the worst jobs to me.

Traveling can be far, far less fun and exciting than most people think. Whether I flew to gigs with the band or sat in the truck with the other roadies, my back ached and I never seemed to get enough sleep. Also, since I had the room next to Finn's, I had to listen as he *kvetched* about my sloth and incompetence.

"The main thing," he told me, "is that they seem to think I'm your babysitter or something, and that means I can't go out chasing women."

"Oh, but you *can*," I retorted. "Don't worry about *me*, sweetie. Just make sure you don't get too friendly with the wrong kinds of women and you end up with HIV."

In Las Vegas, he went cruising on the Strip while I stayed in my room and checked my emails. Wizard was my only friend who knew about this *Punk Off!* gig, and he wanted to know if it was half as much fun as it sounded. I'd hoped for a message from Adnan but knew he still felt bummed at me, and I didn't think I could blame him. Going away on this tour without saying goodbye to him probably was the worst thing for me to do, considering Adnan's feelings of estrangement from me. I checked his blog and found an entry saying, "Sometimes the most painful cuts are made by knives held by one's best friend."

Um, was that a dig at *me*? I mean, who else? Not Wilkie, who followed him around all the time. Those two started getting tight in high school. Adnan and I became little buddies while still toddlers.

Well, that sucked—Adnan had started dissing me online, believing I would never see it, or maybe hoping I would. He seemed to resent my having Queen Bea as my natural mother. Did he think I chose it that way? Your parents, like so many other things in this life, are chosen by God, or the Creator, or whatever you want to call the being who makes the decisions and rules the universe.

Adnan had no right to blame me that, fluke of flukes, the woman of his wet dreams—Queen Bea—turned out to have given birth to me. Still, I empathized with him. He liked and appreciated my empathy. I did, too. I was an experienced empathizer. I really liked that about myself.

I turned off my MacBook Pro and sat in the darkness of my hotel room, contemplating life. Bras, panties and socks lay strewn about. OK, I admit it—I'm a slob. I had just gotten in and already my room was a mess. No worries; the maids would do their thing. In the music world, hotel housekeeping meant as much as booze, babes and bucks.

Suddenly, as I sat up in the darkness, I felt lonelier than I ever had in my entire life. I cupped my hands over my face and cried for the longest time.

CHAPTER 15

Finn told Rudy to pick up Dina Dinner after her set with the Sluts so that she would have some time to sleep before playing with Swarm that evening. But Rudy said to me, "Here, you do it instead," and tossed me the keys. As soon as I got into our rented van, I saw that we were nearly out of gas, so I knew I'd have to fill it up myself and pay with my debit card. I always saved my receipts and hoped that the *Punk Off!* accountants would reimburse me sometime before I retired.

I drove over to the festival site, still mad at Rudy for being too lazy, or stingy, or both, to fill the gas tank before giving me the keys. I still had the taxi receipt from that long drive to the site in southern California, and dreaded the possibility of ultimately eating those little slips of paper that had cost me so much of my own money. I gritted my teeth and sped down the road to collect Dina Dinner. From what I'd heard, she was a terrific replacement for Rings 'n' Things and Swarm liked her, at least to the extent that Swarm liked anyone or anything. Adnan said, "Keep an eye on Dina. She's the Next Big Thing in punk."

Punk Off! had installed a tricked-out trailer at the site for the exclusive use of performers as a place to hang out or sleep. I knocked twice, then threw open the door. Dina lay sprawled on the sofa, topless and cavorting with some naked lovelies. I didn't know many gay people but my attitude was, whatever turns you on.

Dina looked in my direction and said, "Doesn't anyone ever fuckin' knock anymore?"

"I *did* knock. You didn't answer."

"Well, what do you want?"

"I'm here to drive you back to the Hyatt."

Dina glowered at me. "Then wait outside till I'm ready to go."

"Queen Bea told me to make sure that you're all rested and refreshed for your show tonight."

She sat up and pushed away a naked butt. "Did Queen say that? For real?"

To me, the bands of *Punk Off!* were truly a sorry bunch, and it amazed me every day that this festival appealed to so many people. But all these musicians shared one quality I could easily understand—an absolute wish to please Queen Bea. Or at least a desire not to piss her off.

Dina slapped the butt she'd just pushed away. "Later, girlfriends. Gotta see some people and do some shit."

She pulled on some panties. Her ribs stuck out so much that I thought of Auschwitz. She really needed to eat and sleep more. A decent suntan would have helped, too.

Dina fastened her tattered Levi's and said, "Let's go."

"Put on a shirt," I said. "It's illegal for women to go topless. Plus, you'll catch cold."

"Can't remember where I left it." She rooted around a bit, found a black T-shirt with *Punk Off!* emblazoned on the front, and put it on. "Happy now?"

I nodded. "Delighted."

We climbed into the van and I had trouble starting its engine.

"What's the deal?" Dina asked.

"Way low on gas. Need to fill up soon as we can."

"Don't ask me to pay. I'm broke," she said.

"OK, I won't."

We barely made it to a BP station and Dina headed off to the ladies' room while I pumped nearly fifty bucks' worth of unleaded fuel and put the receipt into my wallet. Then I got back in and waited for her.

Ten or fifteen minutes later, Dina had yet to return. I thought, How long does it take to take a piss or drop a deuce?

I sighed, got out of the van and bounded over to the ladies' room. I knocked hard and called out, "Dina? Dina?"

Nothing. Nada.

I thought of Jimi, Jim, Janis, Amy and Kurt—rock stars who had died at twenty-seven. I hated the idea of having Dina added to that list, and discovering her dead on the floor of a BP ladies' can. Throwing open door, I hurried inside and discovered her kneeling on the filthy floor with a rolled-up hundred-dollar bill pressed to one nostril.

I may have been a Libertarian ditz, but I knew something about drugs and Dina definitely had cocaine.

"Dina!—"

She looked up, and just then a blast of afternoon wind blew in and made a cloud of her dope.

"Bitch!" She reared back and threw a poorly aimed hand at me. I stepped aside from it. She lost her balance, fell onto her side, got back up and apparently

96

forgot why she was mad at me. She hugged me. "You want somethin' with me, girlfriend?"

"Yeah, Dina. We gotta go to the hotel."

"How come?"

"Queen said so."

"Oh." I could feel her hand travel around to my left breast. "Nice titties."

"Glad you like 'em."

"We could get into the van and get to know each other a little better."

"Nix. Queen said—"

"'Queen said' don't mean shit to me."

"Well, she's kind of my boss and I wouldn't want to piss her off." Queen was the person who could pay my Stanford bills, and I hadn't even hit her up for that money yet. To spite me, Dina could give Queen a bad report about me and Queen might fire me. A person could never tell what Queen might do.

Just then we heard someone pounding on the door. "Anyone in here?" a woman cried out. "I gotta pee!"

I pulled open the door and shoved Dina Dinner past the woman. Then I exited, too. The woman made this face, as if we were in there being naughty.

The two of us got back into the van, and Dina said, "You hungry? I'm starving. Let's go to Denny's or someplace. I know the perfect way of leaving restaurants without paying, you know. That's why they call me Dina Dinner."

"Maybe next time."

I knocked on Finn's door till my knuckles nearly bled. I heard him call out in a sleepy voice, "What you want?"

"It's me. Christine."

"What you want?" he repeated.

"Need to talk to you."

"Got all day for that."

"I'm worried about Dina Dinner." Even though the carpeting was thick and the walls solid, I feared that my voice was echoing up and down the hallways, overheard by hip people in this cool place. They didn't like snitches. Neither did I.

"She's doing drugs," I called through the door.

"What else is new?" Finn called back.

After a few moments of nothing, I heard the lock click and saw the door swing open. Finn stood before me, dressed in a bulky white bathrobe. His hair stuck out in every direction like a Rastafarian mess, and his face bore scratches or welts.

"Get in here," he muttered.

I did as told.

The bathroom door opened, and out stepped a woman wearing what must have been last night's clothing. She smiled; I smiled back. She couldn't have been more than a few years my senior.

"Christine," said Finn, "this is, um…"

"Teri." She ran a hand through her hair."

"Hey." I offered her a tiny wave.

"So, Finn," said Teri, "you got my passes?"

He snapped his fingers and walked over to his briefcase. After a moment or two of digging and frowning, he pulled out a stack of tickets and handed them to her.

"Awesome!" she said with a squeal as she snapped open her purse and inserted the goodies. She blew him a little kiss and danced out the door.

"As I was saying, Finn, Dina Dinner seems to have a coke problem. I caught her tooting up in the ladies' room."

He covered his mouth with the back of his hand as he yawned. "That so?"

"Yes. And, you know, I'm afraid she'll overdose or get busted or whatever."

"That would be too bad."

"When I barged in on her, her dope blew away. She tried to punch me out."

He looked me up and down. "You're bigger than she is. You could take her in two minutes if it came down to a fight."

I took a deep breath. "She's crazy, man! First she's getting coked up, then she's trying to feel me up, then she's, like, 'Let's go to Denny's and chow down. I'll fake a heart attack or something so we won't have to pay.'"

Finn chuckled.

"Not funny, man," I said.

"Not funny, but amusing. Dina's harmless. You want weird and outrageous? Try knowing Queen Bea twenty years ago. To Queen, thinking it and doing it were pretty much the same thing."

"That sucks," I said.

Finn rubbed his chin. "Christine, I can see that Dina freaked you out, and I'm sorry for that. But you're in her world right now, and drugs are part of that world. Drugs and music go together—they always have. Before Dina, before Queen, before the Beatles and the Stones and Elvis. You know the old saying? 'Sex, drugs and rock 'n' roll.' It's been that way for quite a while."

I nodded that I understood. "Sorry about this,

Finn. I guess that Dina's coke thing is none of my business."

He smirked. "No sweat, girlfriend. Why were you with her, anyway? Rudy was supposed to drive her. He knew what to expect."

"He asked me to do this because, uh, he thought I needed the experience."

"In other words, he was too lazy to get off his ass and do it himself. Tell him I want to speak to him."

Rudy was going to get Finn's boot up his butt in major ways.

CHAPTER 16

The radio switched on and woke me up. Some woman read the news and said, "It's ten o'clock."

My heart pounded. Ten? Rudy set the alarm for eight so we'd be able to check out, have breakfast and leave for Phoenix by nine.

"Rudy—!" I called out above the soft hum of the air conditioner we'd kept on all night at full blast.

Rudy's bed was empty and unmade. His stuff was gone. He'd taken off without me! Bastard! He had changed the alarm as I slept as his way of retaliating after Finn gave him hell over palming off Dina on me.

I called Finn's room but knew he had gone, too. By that time they would be close to Hollywood, where they had agreed to make a personal appearance before heading to LAX.

I got dressed as fast as possible and stuffed my shit into my suitcases and knapsack. I had been a fool to trust Rudy. I knew how much he hated me.

Downstairs, I checked the lobby's restaurant and saw no one from the tour. What could I do? Take Greyhound? When was their next schedule, and how long would it take for that bus to reach my destination?

I had one other option. I hurried out of the hotel, dumped my bags into the trunk of a taxi and said, breathless, "I need to go to the fairgrounds." Thinking that maybe some of the *Punk Off!* semis would still be there and I could catch a ride with one of them.

But no. The big vehicles that carried the heavy equipment from gig to gig had already left. Looking around, I saw the much smaller vehicles that belonged to people who were going to catch each city of the *Punk Off!* tour.

I would have given in to despair except that I recognized a Geo Metro with familiar license plate. I couldn't believe it. Just couldn't.

"Stop the car!" I blurted to the driver.

I stuck my head out the window and yelled, "Chris! Chris Culver!"

I paid the driver, bounded out of the car and collected my things. I walked over to Culver's car, genuinely pleased, for perhaps the first time in my life, to see him.

He gave me a big smile, but I wasn't sure if he was glad to see me or simply amused by my sweaty face, tangled hair and excessive baggage.

"Christine!" he said. "What the hell are you doing out here in the middle of nowhere? Adnan is going to trip when he sees you!"

"Is he here, too?"

He nodded. "This is our summer fun. We're pretending we're Deadheads, following the Grateful Dead from city to city. So, why are *you* here?"

I ran it down for him, and his eyes bulged. "You're with Swarm? For real?"

I nodded. "Don't get too impressed. I'm just a roadie. I do the grunt work with the other fools."

"And where are those other fools?"

I smiled. "I overslept and they sort of booked it out of here without me. I'm stranded and need to get to California. Mind if I ride with you?"

"Get your ass in there."

I loaded some of my stuff into his trunk and said, "There's not enough room for my other suitcase."

He got out, reached into the trunk and pulled out a bungee cord. "We'll tie it to the roof."

As we did, I asked, "Where's Adnan?"

"Droppin' a deuce. He'll be back soon."

A moment later, we got into the car and watched as Adnan came bounding back from the row of portable toilets. He frowned when he noticed that there was now someone in the backseat, then grinned and waved when he saw me.

"Adnan!" Culver exclaimed as soon as my oldest friend plopped into the passenger's seat. "Guess what! Christine is a roadie this summer for Swarm!"

Adnan's face fell. Sleeping in a puny tent and eating junk food three times each day had altered his brain chemistry, and he was fairly moody by nature.

"Oh," he said. "I guess nepotism is alive and well. Must be nice having two mommies, especially when one of them is rich and famous."

I said nothing.

"If you're with the band," he asked, "how come you're hitching a ride with us?"

"Because someone played a practical joke on me and they all took off without me. So, can I ride with you, or what?"

"Looks like you already are," Adnan said.

As we got on the highway and cruised along, with other vehicles honking at us and passing us, Culver asked me myriad questions about Swarm, and gobbled up my stories about Rings' surgery, Maxie's dog and divorce and Dina Dinner's interest in my tits.

As I told these tales, I realized how much I was enjoying sharing my experiences with Culver. I also liked his smiles and laughs as I got to my punch lines. I had always considered myself a gifted, even eloquent raconteur, and I felt grateful to have such an appreciative listener. Alas, Adnan just stared ahead, silent.

"So you've met Dina Dinner, too," Adnan said.

"Who cares?" Culver said. "You've talked about everyone except Queen. Spill it!"

I had very little to spill. I had become acquainted with everyone but Queen Bea. Maybe she was too busy for me, or just didn't want to sit down or hang out and rap with the child she had decided she would rather not raise. Either way, I was damned if I would spill *that* to these two characters sitting up front in this scratched, dented economy car.

"That Queen stuff is kind of personal. I'll tell you another time."

"Sure, whatever," said Culver as he nodded and talked on about Punk Off! and how much fun he was having. "At first Adnan and I were just going to catch a couple of these shows, but when they added Swarm as the headliner? Well, we were, like, 'What the fuck? Let's spend the summer going to *all* their shows!' We'll have college in the fall, but our summer will belong to Swarm, at least as long as our money holds out."

I shrugged, thinking of where I wouldn't be going, and what I wouldn't be doing, in the fall. Right now I was a girl roadie, the victim of a guy roadie's practical joke, forced to bum a ride from high-school friends because my employer had left town as I slept. At the end of the tour, I would ask Queen for Stanford money, and how likely was she to say yes?

It sucked to be me.

"We're stopping at the first place that has wi-fi so I can update my blog," said Adnan, who hadn't said a word in half an hour.

"I'm in kind of a hurry," I said, trying to be difficult. "I'm late. Queen is expecting me."

"Queen probably doesn't know you're absent," said Adnan. "You're a roadie. Not important enough to worry about."

By seven o'clock, we pulled into the campground where the Punk Off! roadies were setting up this and that.

Culver slowed down, and I immediately realized that the thumping on his car's roof had stopped. I stuck my head out the window and looked up.

"We've lost a passenger."

"What?" asked Culver.

"My suitcase. The cord came loose and we lost it somewhere between here and back there."

"Too bad," he said. "Anyway, you dressed for shit most of the time, so it wasn't such a big loss."

"I'll miss my bras, panties and tampons," I said as I climbed out of the car, got what was left of my stuff and said goodbye.

CHAPTER 17

Phoenix was…Phoenix. Ungodly heat and no sign of immediate relief. The city's bosses asked *Punk Off!* to cancel its appearance, but the festival's bosses said nix to that. The beverage sellers ran out of everything by the time Colostomy started its set. Dehydrated fans collapsed faster than paramedics could catch them.

We, the roadies, worked in sweated-through black T-shirts. We snapped at each other; I had trouble pulling my soaking-wet hair away from my face. Even the bands seemed on the rag. I should have guessed from these abysmal conditions that some bad stuff would go down.

As a thank-you gift for the ride out there, I got Adnan and Culver backstage passes. They loved it; even I, no fan of punk, could see how much they loved being back there, wandering around as the musicians tuned their instruments and scratched their asses. Punk Disneyland.

When Queen Bea came in just after sunset, I feared that Adnan might faint as she walked by. He would hardly have been the first; she had that effect on men and women.

As soon as Colostomy finished their set, Maxie Padz called me over to help with her drum kit. She said, "Christine, don't ever get married. Understand? If you do, he'll make you regret it immediately. He'll exploit you in every way, and if someone else comes along who makes him a better offer, he'll split."

Rudy said, "Maxie, don't be so hard on yourself. You're a music legend. You can easily have a man who's worthy of you."

"Yeah, right."

The heat brought out the worst in all of us, especially Kitty Litter, who stood there guzzling from a big bottle of Gatorade.

I gotta drink it for the salt and potassium," she said.

"Drink water instead," Finn retorted. "Gatorade is full of calories, and nobody likes a fat punk rocker."

Finn even got rude with the press, which was totally unlike him. He impressed me as making damn sure that members of the media, who could be Swarm's best friends or worst enemies, received the most courteous treatment possible. One reporter, Doyle from *Phoenix Rising*, started getting a tad bossy, ignoring the tacit rule that press people were *not* band or crew members. But Doyle kept getting in there and giving folks what-for.

"Back off, guy," Finn said to him. "You're just an observer, a reporter. You don't tell us what to do. We let you backstage as a courtesy. We can revoke that courtesy, too. So mind your manners, and don't bug Queen Bea when she's getting psyched up to do her set."

So naturally Doyle approached Queen as she was getting psyched up—legs spread, arms outstretched, face expressionless. Mind and thoughts a zillion miles away.

"Hey, Queen! Barry Doyle from *Phoenix Rising* magazine—" He reached out and clamped a hand over her shoulder.

Queen did her usual thing—she wheeled around and kicked him in the chin with a deftness that Bruce Lee would have envied. Doyle fell back like a cardboard cutout and lay sprawled there.

Finn and I rushed over to the fallen man. Finn shook his head. "Another one bites the dust. I told him not to fuck with her, didn't I?"

"Yes, you did," I said.

"Get one of those paramedics over here. Looks like we got someone in need of attention."

I looked down. "I think he's got a broken nose."

"Probably a concussion, too."

As the paramedics peeled Doyle off the floor, put him on a stretcher and wheeled him past Adnan, my friend looked down at the prostrate man, then looked up at me and gave me his biggest smile with two thumbs up. He'd seen Queen's kick and told me more than once that she had a reputation as the toughest of punk rockers, one of the few women who could take on any man.

Swarm had begun their performance by the time the guys in white took away the silent, bleeding Doyle. The music blaring through the speakers was so relentlessly violent that it seemed a fitting soundtrack to the Phoenix reporter's encounter with Queen.

Dina Dinner's appearance in substitution for Rings 'n' Things thrilled the crowd, as if Robbie Robertson had stepped in to jam with the Who or Ringo Starr had replaced Keith Moon or John Bonham. Mostly, though, to me the music of Swarm just sounded like so much noise. Very loud noise.

It must have sounded that way to the Phoenix police, too, as two officers emerged on stage and wrestled Queen Bea into handcuffs.

I saw a black-clad figure—Adnan—rush out there and jump on a cop's back. Assaulting a police officer was some serious business, so *I* hurried towards the melee and saw Culver running alongside me. Together we pried Adnan off the cop and dragged our friend into the wings.

He kept screaming, "Queen's in trouble! Don't let the bastards kill her!"

From the wings, I saw some fans trying to get over the barricades and climb onto the stage, but the roadies pushed them back. The punks gave up; maybe they thought it was just too damn hot to scuffle with a bunch of big guys who were ready to fight.

Queen didn't exactly resist arrest, but she hardly made the cops' job easier; she just sort of went limp and let the officers carry her into their cruiser. I caught a brief look at her as they eased her into their car. She looked back at me; she rolled her eyes.

"Everything's groovy," Finn said. "I've got Queen's back."

"What did you do for her?" I asked him.

"As soon as she kicked that reporter in the face, I got out my cell phone and made a couple of fast calls to Phoenix attorneys. One will be there at the city jail as soon as Queen gets there."

I frowned. "So you were sort of prepared for something like this to happen."

He laughed. "It happened throughout the 'Eighties, girlfriend. Queen Bea takes no shit from anyone, ever. Guys or chicks tried to grab her ass or tits, she'd knock them down. She'd get busted, we'd get a lawyer, problem solved."

"Well," I said, "at least let me go with you to the police station."

He shook his head. "I'm not going. We pay lawyers to go to police stations and post bail bonds and get people out of jail. That way, people like you and me can go back to our hotel, eat dinner and go to bed."

We returned to our hotel but I did not sleep. Instead, since my room had a view of the lobby, I sat at the window, waiting for Queen Bea to appear. At three in the morning, Rudy staggered in.

"Dammit, I wish they would find you your own room," he said.

"They will as soon as they can. I don't like this arrangement much, either." Then, "Queen hasn't shown up yet."

"Naw, they'll keep in her lockup till morning. They love doing that to famous folks—it teaches celebrities a lesson about fuckin' with the Man."

I called Finn.

"You know what time it is, Christine?"

"Rudy says they're keeping Queen till morning."

"Yeah. They don't want to wake a judge just to get his signature for her release."

"But you said she'd be released immediately."

"Oh, well. I don't guess a night in jail will kill her. She's been locked up overnight before. Maybe they'll even give her breakfast before they let her go."

Click.

Thanks, dickhead. Now I feel so much better.

I turned on the TV but kept the volume on low so Rudy could sleep. CNN was running its recycled stories, but at the bottom I found the scroll PUNK QUEEN ARRESTED FOR ASSAULT IN

PHOENIX FACES YEARS IF CONVICTED.

With a heavy heart and racing pulse I called Finn again but got his voicemail. I stared at the TV for several minutes, wondering how Finn and Rudy could sleep—Rudy, ten feet away, snored like a foghorn—when they surely knew that Queen could serve years for kicking that reporter. Even if they were indifferent to her as a human being, weren't they worried about losing their meal ticket? Rings 'n' Things had disappeared, replaced by Dina Dinner, and most fans, if anything, liked the change? But Swarm without Queen Bea? *Punk Off!* without her? No way. Forget it.

Maybe the reason Finn and Rudy were so cavalier about Queen's current predicament was that she wasn't their mother. She was mine, and I was her kid, even though we scarcely knew each other. She needed my support, and I was going to provide it.

I got my handbag and left the hotel. Outside, I went up to the first taxi and asked its driver, "Where would the police take someone to spend the night before their arraignment?"

"I'll take you there," he said.

I nodded and climbed in. He drove me to a big old stone building that looked out of place in Phoenix. Or maybe it fit right in, but I didn't know that because my knowledge of Phoenix was very limited and my knowledge of police stations came mainly from *Hill Street Blues* and *Law and Order*.

I went inside and they told me they were holding nobody named Queen Bea. But then one clerk confirmed that Beatrix P. Spurl would be arraigned in Courtroom 10 at nine that morning.

I checked the wall clock: 5:02. I walked down one hallway and then another until I found Courtroom 10.

What would be the point of spending more money on a taxi back to the hotel, where I would lay in bed and worry for a few hours before returning to the courthouse?

I sat on the bench outside Courtroom 10 and spend the next hours fretting and nodding off. Once or twice I sprawled out and nearly got a decent nap except that a couple of cops roused me for a pat-down. They asked what business I had there. When I told them about Queen Bea, they searched me some more.

From five till eight, the courthouse had been silent. By eight-thirty, the rest of the place slept on but Courtroom 10 woke up and got busy. Reporters, cameramen and countless others jammed the hallway, looking at me as if I were part of the riff raff awaiting arraignment that morning.

I sat up before anyone tried to sit on me. Then I slid over to the edge of the bench and refused to get up for the suits who scowled at me and wanted to sit down.

I probably would have failed to enter the courtroom, too, but Finn showed up with half a dozen lawyers who pushed, shoved and body blocked a path for me.

The judicial system took its time, too. Every small-time offender in town faced the judge before the main event occurred.

"The People versus Beatrix Spurl," shouted the bailiff.

The room suddenly brightened up with flashes of camera light, as if we were at a Hollywood premiere. Queen Bea stood up, still in her black stage suit, stifling a yawn and tucking a stray wisp of blonde hair behind her ear. Her lawyers muttered a few words, the judge said even less before grabbing her gavel and setting Queen free.

The reporters' questions, all asked at once, came at her in an incomprehensible barrage. She shrugged and yelled, "One at a time, you idiots!"

The judge scowled and used her gavel again. "Take it outside! Leave immediately!"

Queen and the reporters did just that. I waved at her; she stared and sneered into the cameras. The questions continued out into parking lot.

"Queen, how do you think that reporter felt about being kicked in the face by you?"

"You should ask him as soon as he comes out of his coma."

I climbed onto a big potted plant and watched them from about twenty feet away, feeling like the world's biggest fool. Why had I spent so much of the night on that wooden bench outside the courtroom worrying about Queen Bea? Finn had already told me that she was likely to treat her arrest and night in jail as one big joke.

Soon the Phoenix heat overcame me and I got off the potted plant. I found a place under a palm tree and dozed off. I woke up, or was shaken awake, and when I opened my eyes I saw no reporters or anyone else but Queen Bee.

"Hey," she said, "you've got to wake up and get your shit together."

"I don't want to. I just want to go home." I wiped away a tear as I got to my feet and followed her to the limousine.

"You've got to take better care of yourself," she said as we got into the big, air-conditioned car.

Finn sat smirking as we made ourselves comfortable. "Christine spent several hours on that bench outside the courtroom because she was so worried about you."

Queen snarled and pointed her finger at him. "What's your problem, dude? We promised her people that we'd look out for her and make sure she wouldn't have to deal with this kind of bullshit."

"Did you want Rudy to handcuff her to her bed?" he asked.

"Hey," I said. "I was watching TV and CNN said that Queen could do serious time for kicking that guy."

"CNN," Queen Bea muttered. After several long, awkward moments, she added, "Look, Christine, let me explain something to you. Finn and I know exactly what we're doing. We've been doing this for a long time. So if Finn says, 'Everything's cool,' you can believe him, even if CNN says I'm going to be executed at sundown. I did my night in jail, I smiled at the judge, I answered the reporters' questions. It's all a done deal. Understand?"

I nodded.

Queen stuck her thumb in my direction and said to Finn, "She genuinely cares about me. How come you don't?"

He laughed and said, "Because she's a loving person. She wouldn't last fifteen minutes in the music business. She's too decent."

I smiled. If only they knew about the money I wanted to get out of her. Would they still think I was such a loving, caring kid?

CHAPTER 18

I got back to the hotel just as Rudy started giving us roadies our assignments.

"Next stop, Albuquerque," he said. "We leave at ten-thirty. Christine, don't go to sleep. You wouldn't want to be left behind again, right?"

"Right."

"By the way, you must have had your iPhone off because some woman called the hotel and said she was your mother. I told her you were spending the night in jail with Queen."

I wanted to punch him out, but he was twice my size, so I took out my iPhone and called home. I had done so several times since my adventure began, and our conversations had been terse and awkward. My father hinted at the Stanford money, to which I had replied, "Not yet." I swore my mother was doing a crossword puzzle as she asked about my general well-being.

This time, things were a bit different. *What's happening over there? Why were you and that woman in jail?*

"Mom," I said in an even tone of voice, "it was nothing. Seriously."

"Oh, I would say that a night in jail is *something*."

"I wasn't in jail. Queen was. They let her out."

"The news said she could go to prison for years."

"The news lies," I told her. They let her out. It was

just a big joke for publicity."

"And you became a victim of that 'joke for publicity.' Since when is being arrested ad put in jail a 'joke'? That lifestyle is no good for you, Christine. I don't want that awful woman dragging you down with her."

Mom was right about Queen's lifestyle—that punk goddess freaked *me* out, too. But I also knew what I needed to do for myself.

"I'm completing this tour, Mom. I'm not coming home."

I would stay on the *Punk Off!* tour, and not just because I planned to ask Queen Bea for money. Not because I thought that this punk-rock tour was such a big deal, either. I wanted to do it because my job as a roadie was hard, honest, real work. My parents had always done their best to shelter me; what had my life been thus far? School, hanging out with Adnan, eating and sleeping—even Stanford, if I made it there, would be a vacation from real life. At times I felt seventeen going on seven. How could I walk away from this opportunity to grow up?

"I wonder about you, Christine," Mom said as I pressed my iPhone to my ear so that nobody could overhear. "Why would you want to have anything to do with that woman?"

Well, Mom, I wanted to say, she and I do have a few things in common—DNA, for one.

That evening, I received an email from Wizard:

Adnan says he and Culver had to drive you to a gig because the other roadies left you behind. What's up with *that?*

I thought for a moment about the two Phoenix cops and the onstage tussle. Had Adnan blogged about jumping on the cop's back? If so, did he do so accurately? It would be just like him to exaggerate and bullshit.

Wizard's email included a link to Adnan's blog. But I wasn't in the mood for Adnan just then, so I didn't even bother to read what he'd written.

If Queen Bea had been punk's "live fast, love hard, die young" poster chick in the 1980s, Dina Dinner was its new Queen. As *Punk Off!* lumbered like a hippopotamus on the freeway towards Denver, I began to realize that Dina Dinner's ladies'-room antics were just Dina being herself. Queen said, "Dina is twenty-one, and she think she'll die at twenty-seven, like Janis Joplin and Amy Winehouse. Dina's life's goal seems to be to pack as many good times as she can into those few years she thinks she has left."

I wondered about Queen's secret to relative longevity. Wasn't she the woman who crashed a motorbike through a plate-glass window and walked away, laughing about it?

Oddly, Queen showed very little interest in partying during *Punk Off!* While Maxie, Kitty and Finn did tequila shots each night and bragged about their hangovers the morning after, Queen stayed in her hotel room—she had an entire set of rooms to herself—and, Finn said, watched cable TV. I suppose she had gotten her fill of carousing during the 1980s. She had certainly ridden her share of dicks back then.

I was the result of one of her sexual encounters.

Denver, Dina's birthplace, was the city from which she had escaped several years earlier. As Swarm's temporary guitarist, she pretended to be the Mile High City's favorite daughter who had come back in a blaze of glory. She sat next to Queen during interviews, and as soon as the sun disappeared behind the Rockies, she staggered into one Denver nightspot after another, cadging drinks from well-wishers.

Dina drove around town in her Hummer, packed with friends from her Denver high school. The locals all said that their city's finest nightspot was the Bakery, a bread-and-cakes factory that had been put out of business by a national chains and converted into a dance club. As we approached it, we saw over a hundred people standing in line behind a velvet rope.

"Long lineup," I said.

"Not for us," retorted Dina Dinner.

Just behind us, a taxi stopped. We got out, and I saw a big furry head sticking out of the window.

Finn scowled. "Maxie, why's that fur-ball here?"

The Swarm drummer got out of the taxi. She had her Saint Bernard on a leash. "I couldn't leave him in the hotel. He gets separation anxiety." She turned to Kitty Litter. "Why did you bring all that junk food to rehearsal? Bernie ate most of it. He might vomit."

"Junk food?" Finn spun towards Kitty. "Why did you bring junk food to a rehearsal? You're getting as big as a house!"

Kitty shrugged. "Doesn't matter. The dog got most of it."

Finn shook his head. "You've got to find a place to put him. We can't take a dog into a nightclub."

But the Bakery's management was only too happy

to let Bernie in.

The place seemed like a warehouse with lots of spinning lights, loud music and flailing limbs. The dancers wore what I immediately recognized as what passed for haute couture in the Rocky Mountain State—Gap and Banana Republic jeans and Oxford shirts. The mindless disco beat soon irritated me.

Kitty Litter mouthed at me, *Yuck!*

I nodded and mouthed back, *Go somewhere else?*

Kitty shrugged. She mouthed, *Finn likes it.*

The Bakery was full of beautiful women. At least a dozen of them surrounded Bernie, scratching his stomach and stroking his ears. I sat nearby and watched as Finn, all smiles at the sight of all those sexy young women and the object of their adoration, went up to Maxie Padz.

"Go dance, Maxie. I'll hang out with the boy for a while."

Our party comprised Dina and her friends, plus some of the *Punk Off!* band members. Dina held court in one of the lounges, knocking back tequila shots and telling everyone how great it was being Dina Dinner.

I stood watching them for a few minutes and thought back to my years in high school and the dangers of peer pressure. Now I beheld Maxie Padz and Kitty Litter, two middle-aged multimillionaires, as they tried to outdrink Dina Dinner and her buds. Maxie ended up falling down drunk onto a sofa.

I tried to shake her awake. Nothing doing.

"Dumb bitch," I muttered.

"What's the problem?" asked Rudy.

"She's fucked up. I'll fetch Finn."

"No, I'll get him. Kitty's been gorging on *hors*

d'oeuvres. Go find her somewhere to barf."

I led Kitty out of the Bakery and into the parking lot, away from the street lights. She bent over double a few times and made some truly disgusting noises, but after several minutes shook her head and said, "I can't do it."

"Let's go back to the hotel," I said.

"Like fuck," she said. "Let's go party some more."

So we did. Actually, Kitty did; I went to the Rite-Aid down the block to get some stomach medicine for the next time the girls went out partying. Kitty made it back into the Bakery with no questions asked; I, Christine Slanz, also known as Miz Nobody, was prevented from reentering the nightspot. Finally, one of our entourage came to the door and vouched for me.

When I got back to our little section of the Bakery, I saw Kitty devouring more goodies and Maxie was fidgeting on the sofa while mumbling to herself. Finn sat near Maxie with a petite blonde on his lap. He had his hand on her ass and his tongue down her throat.

"Finn! Where's Bernie?" I asked him.

He withdrew his tongue. "Dunno."

"Where's his leash?"

"Search me."

"You said you'd look after him."

"Go look for him." Finn slipped his tongue back into the girl's mouth.

I looked past him and spotted Bernie. The big pooch, on his hind legs, lapping up a tray of something. I hurried over and grabbed him from behind. Then I felt a hand clamp down on a big hank of my hair.

"Not supposed to have dogs in here," shouted the

bouncer over the din of the disco thump-thump-thump. "It's against the law."

"But one of you guys let him in here," I shouted back. "He's not mine. I'm just looking after him."

The bouncer might have dragged me out of there by my locks except that some of Dina's buds chose that moment to show her that they, too, could be badasses.

A couple or three of them jumped on the bouncer's back, pounding him as Dina cheered them on. The Bakery had too many people—inebriated, perspiring, aggressive folks—and while I wouldn't say a melee started, the pushing and shoving sent many guests onto their backsides.

Presently someone pulled the fire alarm, but it sounded no worse than the disco racket, so at first most of us thought of it as a sound effect. Then the disc jockey stopped the music and everyone scrambled away before the pigs arrived.

I'm still unsure as to who drove Dina's Hummer back to the hotel, because Dina was too stoned to walk. Maxie and Kitty were fucked up, too. I watched as the vehicles' doors opened and our gang stepped out or exited in the arms of this or that roadie. The bunch of them headed into the hotel's lobby. I remembered that we had forgotten one of us.

Bernie.

The big dog was still at the Bakery.

"Finn!" I called out.

"Hush. I'm standing right behind you." He stepped around to face me.

"Oh. The dog's not here."

"I know. We left him at the Bakery."

"What'll Maxie say when she discovers her dog is

missing?"

He shrugged. "Maxie is in no shape to notice much of anything right now. In the morning, we'll deal with the missing dog."

"You don't seem to be taking this very seriously."

Finn smirked. "I'm taking it as seriously as it deserves to be taken."

"What's that supposed to mean?"

"Just what I said. We forgot the dog at the nightclub. The dog has a collar and an ID tag. The Bakery's management knows it's Maxie's dog. They'll call her in the morning and say, 'Come get your fuckin' mutt.' Any questions?"

"Yeah. How come, with Maxie's divorce and other personal issues, you just don't give a shit about her? Wouldn't it bother you if her dog ended up getting killed tonight because we didn't take enough responsibility for him?"

"Kiss my ass!"

My blood ran cold. His cold tone was a new thing, especially when directed at me. Up till then, he had been my good buddy, full of smiles and pats on the back. He had simply run out of patience with me.

"Listen, you ugly bitch," he added, "the only reason I put up with you is that Queen said I should. But I don't like you and never will. You work for me, not the other way around. You do as I say. Understand?"

The chick from the Bakery tapped his shoulder and cleared her throat. "Finn, I'm getting lonely."

He nodded and they walked towards the hotel's elevator.

I wandered around the lobby for quite some time, disoriented. Finn would punch me out if I bothered him again. Maxie would be hung over for the next few days and therefore of no use to me or anyone else. Rudy didn't like me, period. He was afraid of Finn. But I felt such anxiety over Bernie and what might happen to him that I had to get someone involved in the dog's return.

My options were limited. So I went to the top dog, so to speak.

CHAPTER 19

The hotel had nobody registered as Queen Bea, so I tried Spurl, and it worked. For whatever reason, Queen hadn't given me her iPhone number, so I had to call her through the hotel, and that was a hassle.

"Hello?" She sounded as wrecked as Maxie.

"Queen, it's Christine."

"Why you callin'? Is there a problem?" She sounded more mentally together now.

"Well, yes. We left Bernie at the Bakery last night."

"Who the fuck is Bernie?"

"Maxie's big dog." I ran it all down for him— Bernie's unlawful admission to the nightclub, Maxie's decision to get wasted and the fight that started once the bouncer grabbed me by the hair.

"What's Finn got to say about all this?"

"Not much. He picked up some chick and they're getting it on as we speak. Rudy's no help, either. What'll we do?"

Queen said nothing for the longest time. Perhaps I had made a mistake in saying, "What'll we do?" To her, it must have seemed as if I were saying, *Maxie made a mistake in bringing her dog along. I made a mistake in saying I would look after the dog. Now, Queen, I'm trying to drag you into this and make our mistakes yours, too.* She paid very little mind to the absence of Rings 'n' Things once Finn had brought in Dina Dinner to replace Rings. The fact that Dina was a far better musician than Rings simply added to Queen's indifference. Plus, Queen's personal philosophy was pretty much, "If it's your problem, don't make it mine."

Finally, she said, "Give me a few minutes to throw something on. Meet me in the lobby."

I had a hard time believing she was going to meet with me. But then I heard the elevator doors open and out she stepped, tugging at her studded-leather jacket and jeans. Then she smoothed out her hair and flashed me a pretty blonde smile.

"Here," she said, handing me the keys to one of the half-dozen vehicles we had rented. "You drive. I'd love to, but the judge took away my license years ago.

I nodded and we got into the minivan. I felt strangely nervous, driving as Queen Bea sat in the passenger's seat. It was as if I were a student driver and she the examiner, and she would fail me if I didn't drive recklessly enough. When we arrived at the Bakery, some cars were still there.

"I guess some of the staff are still there," I said. "Maybe they're looking after Bernie for us."

I stood at the front door, pounding away until a petite female opened it. I looked past her and saw bouncers and whatnot cleaning up.

"Hate to bug you, but we're looking for a lost dog—"

"No dogs in here," she said. "It's against the law."

"It's Maxie Padz's Saint Bernard. You let him in last night. I guess he got out after the fire alarm sounded and everyone split—"

Then she noticed the tall blonde woman standing next to me.

"*Queen Bea!*" Her eyes bulged. "From Swarm? Oh, wow! You know, we've had Britney and Madonna and Bono here, but you! This is *too* awesome!"

By then, of course, everyone who had been sweeping and cleaning stood at the door, wanting to know what all the excitement was about.

"Hey," Queen said with a casual wave, as if she'd had people fawn over her throughout her adult life. "We're here to get the doggie so we can go home and get some sleep."

"No dogs here, Queen," said the petite lady. "You're welcome to come in and have a look."

We did, and found no Bernie. We went back to the front door and Queen said, "I guess he's out there, wandering the streets of Denver."

Back in the minivan, Queen shook her head. "I have no idea why Maxie insists on taking that dog everywhere. It's just one hassle after another."

So we did the only thing that was left to do: We drove up and down the streets of the city, calling Bernie's name.

"Berrrrneeeee!" Queen shrieked into the Denver night.

"What's 'burning'? Where's the fire?" someone called out from the darkness.

"Just looking for a dog named Bernie," Queen shouted back.

"If there's no fire, shut the fuck up!" retorted the voice.

"Your turn now," Queen said to me.

"Huh?"

"Call out the dog's name."

"I can't. Not like the way you did."

"Sure you can. Just think of something that really bugs you and get loud. Pretend you're screaming at your worst enemy."

Easy to do. In my mind I formed a composite of all the people I felt had done me wrong in some big or small way, then I made that person into a green evil being with warts out of which sprouted gray hairs.

I stuck my head out the window and roared, *"BERRRNEEEE!"*

I looked over at Queen. She gave me the thumbs up. "You may just have a future in punk rock."

"Is that all punk's about? You just scream and sound enraged?"

She shrugged. "Mostly, yes. Punk bands are mainly a bunch of talentless guys and chicks who really want to be in bands. The thing is, punk rock is about anger. Punks are angry people. We come of age, all of us, and we look around at the world. Some look at the world and see opportunity. Others look at the world and see it as a really fucked-up place, full of bullshit and hypocrisy. And the worst part of it is, the people with the power to put things right want to keep things fucked up!" She sighed and paused. "I guess that's at the heart of punk, the music and culture. Rage against an unfair world."

"Is that how Swarm got started? A bunch of angry young women?"

"That's how all punk got started. That's how rock music got started. A bunch of poor black kids, poor white kids. The ones who get rich don't know how to cope with money, so they drink it and drug it all away."

I thought for a few moments and said, "I'm having a little trouble picturing Kitty, Rings and Maxie as being wild, crazy and angry like you. They seem like nice enough middle-aged suburban women,

127

but you've still got that edge."

"No, they're still edgy and angry, just like me. The money hasn't softened us. We're all still deeply dissatisfied with the state of the world and the cruelty people exhibit towards each other. If we'd gotten complacent, we would never have agreed to this *Punk Off!* thing."

"You still wear leathers and drive a motorcycle," I said. "I'll bet people freak out if they have leaded windows."

She grimaced. "Yeah, that. People still say, 'She's the chick who drove her bike through that lawyer's window.' Just like when Keith Moon used to blow up toilets in the hotels the Who stayed in. But that lawyer? He deserved it. He was so smug and condescending, ripping us off and lying about it, thinking we couldn't do anything to him in retaliation. He was disbarred, you know. Serves him right."

"That must have been an extraordinary day for you," I said.

She nodded. "Especially when I got off the bike and walked away from all those glass shards. They took me to the hospital against my will. No cuts, no shock, no nothing. It was like the Man Upstairs was saying, 'Next time you drive your bike through glass, I'm not gonna save your ass.'"

"Sounds to me like you were just standing up for yourself."

"I was not someone who deserved to be emulated. I wrecked plenty of equipment, cars, bikes, homes. Lots of times I was high on dope." She smirked. "Maybe that's one of the things you're supposed to say when you're trying to learn about being someone's mother: 'Don't do the things that I did.'"

128

I laughed. "Don't sweat it. My, uh, parents already gave me the 'Just say no' rap a few dozen times. At my high school, all drugs are available every day. The local dealers, who are my classmates, will come up and say, 'If you want drugs, come and see me. I'll get you whatever you want.' Then he'll shake my hand, like it's a business deal or something. Myself, I have other interests."

"You mean like politics? The Young Libertarians?"

I frowned. "Yeah! How did you know?"

"Because I checked you out online. Everyone seems to have a MacBook Pro or iPad or something now, so I got one. It's sort of my new addiction."

"I got kicked out of that Young Libertarians thing. I sort of was involved in this scandal. They said I was cheating with another kid on a big exam we were doing in the school cafeteria."

"But you weren't cheating. It was just a big misunderstanding."

I couldn't tell if she was defending or mocking me.

"Well, I'm not sure if I was or wasn't. Anyway, the principal was, like, 'Just blame it on the other kid, we'll expel him and you'll walk.'"

"You should have said, 'OK, it was all his fault.'"

I said nothing. Neither did she. I was a libertarian with a social conscience and she was, well, Queen Bea. I wanted this conversation to stop. We were getting too personal, especially about me and my immediate future, and if we kept talking, she might need an entire fifteen minutes to figure out that I had graduated from high school, been accepted at Stanford and now needed her assistance in financing my formal education.

We instantly changed the subject as we watched a truck roll by with the words ANIMAL CONTROL painted on its side and knew we had found Bernie. We followed the vehicle for a mile or so until it pulled into a Denny's parking lot. Its driver exited the vehicle and headed into the restaurant. We got out of the minivan and approached the truck.

"Bernie?" Queen said in a soft voice.

We heard a soft, deep bark.

"We've come to get you," Queen said. "Shame on you for leaving the Bakery. You're supposed to stay close to your humans."

I tried the door. "Unlocked."

Queen smiled. "Sweet."

We opened the door, reached in and dragged the Saint Bernard out of the vehicle. We carried him over to our minivan and pushed him in. He traipsed in a few feet, curled up and went to sleep.

Queen and I crawled in, too, and I started the engine. "Home, sweet home," I murmured.

"That's another thing about my line of work," she said. "I don't really have a home. Oh, I have a place to stow my shit and get my mail, but I'm no more *at* home there than I am in these hotels."

"Your life," I said, "still looks like fun to me."

She and I cruised back to the hotel in nonexistent traffic as the sun rose. I thought that after our night of partying at the Bakery, everyone would have gone upstairs and conked out. But no; Maxie Padz sat in the lobby's luxurious coffee shop, feeding slabs of ham to a Saint Bernard.

"Hey," Maxie said, looking a bit tired but otherwise fine. "Didn't know you had a dog, too."

"We don't," Queen said. "We thought this was

Bernie."

Maxie laughed. "Well, as you can see, Bernie is sitting here having breakfast with Mama."

"I guess we went out and got the wrong dog," I said.

"Guess so," said Maxie. "Did you know that Bernie actually walked from the Bakery to here all by himself? I told him, as soon as he got here, that he should never wander off by himself again."

Queen said, "Well, now you have two dogs."

Maxie guffawed. "Did you *really* think that was Bernie. Can't you tell that the one you found is female?"

Queen let out a big yawn and said, "All this excitement has worn me out. Gotta go upstairs and get my beauty sleep." She headed off towards the elevator.

I followed her and said, "Queen, I'm sorry about this. I shouldn't have bugged you and gotten you out of bed for this."

She threw back her head and laughed. "First off, you didn't do anything to me. I got out of bed; it was my own decision. Second, that was fun! I hadn't done any crazy shit in a while." He added, "Now, when I get to my room, I'm gonna sleep until noon or later. Don't wake me unless the hotel's on fire."

The elevator doors opened and he stepped inside. I watched the doors close and thought, What the hell are we going to do with that dog?

CHAPTER 20

The stress of her divorce was getting Maxie completely weirded out. "I'm not getting on that flight to Kansas City," she declared. "Terrorists might shoot the plane down. I'll ride with Rudy in the equipment truck. I don't care if it takes eleven hours."

I was OK with that; it meant I would use her first-class air ticket. Rudy got pissed about it. "If Christine's not riding with me, who the fuck's gonna help me unload all that shit?"

"I'll help you when we get to the concert site in Kansas City," I told him.

The final say about my flying to Kansas City came from Queen Bea, which meant that it was a done deal. By then, everyone knew that I had a special relationship with the boss lady, which meant I was something more than just a roadie. My peculiar status prevented Rudy from treating me as a second-class citizen. Sometimes I actually pitied the fool. He spent so much time chasing women, and so little actually making it with them, that he needed to take out his frustrations on me, the only female he could pick on with impunity. Until now.

Rudy wasn't the only one on the rag as *Punk Off!* headed east. Finn got mad because he had to pay someone to adopt that Saint Bernard Queen and I abducted from Denver Animal Control. Kitty Litter was angry at some music reviewer who had mocked her bubble butt in his online column.

Finn said, "I'm going to bring in a dietitian to keep

you girls lean and mean."

Rings 'n' Things had emailed Swarm to say that she had been discharged from the hospital and sent home to complete her recuperation. She wrote, "I'm looking forward to continuing with *Punk Off!* when it goes overseas…"

"Rings is out, Dina Dinner is in," pronounced Finn. "I'll have to call Rings and give her the bad news."

Everyone seemed to have some sort of grievance. The Menstrual Cramps, Dina's other band, started complaining that it was really hard to get gigs at home in Los Angeles without their much-celebrated guitarist. The members of Colostomy were scarcely speaking to each other, and Ebola had started to think that they, and not Swarm, should be the festival's headliner.

Queen said, "Touring is a bitch."

She alone seemed to bicker with no one and go through daily life without conflicts or disputes, just as years earlier she had traded all-night booze-and-dope binges for quiet evenings with her MacBook Pro. At first I thought her detachment might be due to the fact that, as the star of *Punk Off!* she avoided other people's melodramas and bullshit simply because she could. But then I started to think she was aloof and detached because she'd been born that way.

In front of an audience, Queen was as fiery and animated as ever, throwing kicks and karate chops at the invisible green behemoths of greed and hypocrisy as if she were back in 1985, a beautiful young woman enraged by the ugly world she was forced to live in.

She started reviling Obama and his years as president, and suddenly, for me at least, the

Midwestern heat turned cold, and it turned cold because so much of what she said about him came from my libertarian blog entries. She had checked me out, not because she wanted to get to know me better, but because she needed new material to deliver onstage.

I supposed she was just being a professional, giving her audience what she thought it wanted. I was a professional, too. I had given Queen what she thought she wanted, and I hadn't asked her for anything in return. Yet.

As *Punk Off!* went east, and then north, the audiences grew meaner and more demanding…or maybe we were just getting tired and cranky. By the time we reached Chicago, the crowds turned out in vast numbers, but they stood out there in the rain and mud, and the bands fretted about whether they could perform well enough to hold the fans' attention and distract them from the abysmal conditions. The onus to make punk-rock history, as it were, inevitably was on Swarm. They did what they needed to do, but it became increasingly difficult. Dina Dinner, of course, could jump around like a 20-year-old David Lee Roth, but Kitty Litter and Maxie Padz groaned like old women after each set. Even Queen Bea looked spent.

Adnan sent me a text message: *They're still great and I love them all, but they better not disappoint me.*

I hadn't seen him since that lovely evening in Phoenix when he jumped on that cop's back. I texted Culver, *That evening in Phoenix? You and I saved Adnan from getting busted, so how come he's pissed at me and not at you?*

Culver replied, *Go figure Adnan.*

I said, *I can't figure him out. Lord knows I've tried. I've known him since we were babies but still can't understand how his mind works.*

Well, he said, *here's an insight for you. Queen had belonged to him, so to speak, for many years, then he discovered that you were her bio-daughter. That was some seriously heavy shit for her to deal with.*

Culver, I wrote, *that's because Adnan chooses to see things that way. He can choose to let my bio-relationship with Queen be a non-issue.*

Like hell he can, Christine.

I felt they were both angry at me, so to put things right between us, I got them backstage passes for the Milwaukee show. At least they got out of the heavy rain. Our site, a big fairground, could have doubled as a mud-wrestling ring. The hot, humid day was marred by the clouds of bugs swirling about until killed by the countless zappers installed at the sides of the stage. When the bands took their breaks, the sounds of electrocuted insects became much too audible.

The bands played their very best that day, as if to compensate their fans for enduring all the bugs, rain and mud.

By that time, Maxie had begun taking the greatest care of her drums, practically handling them with kid gloves so she could abuse them on stage. She had concluded that the only people she could trust with her equipment were Rudy and me. I wanted to say to her, "Please, Maxie, don't trust me. I'm not worthy."

They kept me busy for hours backstage, so I didn't meet up with Adnan until minutes before Swarm's set. I nearly had a heart attack when I saw him—if he hadn't been standing next to Culver, I'm sure I would have failed to recognize him.

A couple of weeks on the road, far away from home and high school, had changed—improved? matured?—into someone new. His famous aversion to sunlight had kept his skin as pallid as a ghost's; now, after many days in the open air, he had a deep, rich tan. He had stopped dyeing his hair and now his dark-blond roots had begun to show. He'd also shitcanned his ghoulish black apparel—Culver had obviously taken him to the Gap or Banana Republic and outfitted him with khaki shorts and a light-blue T-shirt.

I stared and stared. I drooled, too. He looked so hot, fine and sexy. When had I ever felt that way about Adnan?

He mocked by bulging eyes and said, "I should take a picture of you and put it online. You'd never live it down."

"It's just that you look so…so…"

Just then a deep voice said into the microphone, *"Ladies and gentlemen, Wretched recording artists Swarm!"*

The racket started and the three of us—Adnan, Culver and I—stood and listened as if we were in church, taking in sacred choral music. I decided that as soon as Swarm finished up, I would introduce these two to the band. Especially Culver, who had been a true friend lately, much more so than Adnan. They weren't exactly kin to me, but did I really have any? I had never met my bio-daddy; my bio-mama, onstage singing at that moment, hadn't really said whether she wanted anything to do with me; my adoptive parents were really just good-natured folks who had taken me in. I didn't belong to the punk world and it didn't have much interest in me, either.

For the moment, all the family I had were the two kids standing next to me.

Queen, usually too exhausted after her set to meet fans or the media, wiped the sweat off her hands and shook Adnan's and Culver's.

"Adnan," she said, "were you the guy who jumped on a cop in Phoenix during our set?"

He blushed and nodded. "I've listened to you all my life. Your music means so much to me. I've played your songs thousands of times."

Queen Bea smirked. "I'm surprised you're not brain-dead by now."

To my amazement, Queen stayed there and continued the conversation. Normally she had no patience for the blah-blah-blah of everyday conversation. "Over the years," she had told me, "I've answered so many trivial question so many times that I now refuse to do that." Whenever she believed she had said everything worth saying, and heard everything worth hearing, she was totally OK with walking away right then and there. If the other person was offended, well, too bad for them.

"So, Adnan," she was saying, "what are you going to do this fall? Got a college picked out?"

My jaw dropped. In the brief time I had known Queen Bea, I could have counted, on the fingers of half a hand, the number of times she had shown sincere interest in another person. So why was she now asking about Adnan's future?

Then I figured it out: She was asking the sorts of questions a mom would ask her daughter's beau. It truly astounded me that she clearly thought he was my boyfriend and she was acting like an actual mom. Who woulda thunk?

She was nice to Culver, too. He opened his yap and said, "Queen, I never thought you would look so old!"

Queen introduced Adnan and Culver to the rest of the band, and those women were courteous to my friends. Even Finn smiled and said hidy. He had been angry at me since Queen and I had boosted that dog from the truck, but he had no beefs with Adnan or Culver, and he even invited them to the after-concert party being hosted by Colostomy's new recording label.

Finger Wave Records had rented the entire top floor of the hotel, and their bash was, well, stupendous. Frankly, I was getting jaded by the whole rock 'n' roll party scene, but had fun observing Adnan as he took it all in. For him and Culver, this party wasn't quite as fantastic as hanging out with U2 or Springsteen, but it exposed them to more rock-star glamor than they had ever experienced. Finn had decided to spend the evening introducing them to some of the people there.

"Hey," said Rudy as he plopped down on the sofa next to me. "Must be nice to have mamas in high places, huh?"

"Rudy," I retorted, "I really hope you get laid tonight. If you can get some of that pubic fuzz off your brain, it might make you a better person."

"If you can get Queen Mama to buy you a nose job," he said, "it might make you a *prettier* person."

"I'll be sure and tell her you said that." I then became distracted by the sight of Finn talking to Adnan. Culver had wandered off to yak it up with the members of Colostomy. "Have I," I asked Rudy, "ever used my relationship with Queen to get out of doing dirty work?"

Rudy let out a bitter little laugh. "Your whole involvement in this tour is a joke. I do ten times as much as you, and I've had to break my ass for years to get to be the head roadie."

He got more pissed by the moment, but I ignored him. Finn was getting much too friendly with Adnan, whispering in his ear and rubbing his shoulder. I didn't think my old friend had a gay bone in his body, but one never knew about Finn—maybe that dude was into everything. I wasn't going to let him get into Adnan, that was for freakin' sure.

CHAPTER 21

I wanted to march right over there and punch Finn in the nose. I really did.

I had tried to be nonjudgmental about him, Queen and all these other folks who surrounded me on this tour. Rock 'n' roll always seemed to shout, "If it feels good, do it!" While that wasn't my particular credo, I tried to respect the rights of those who did the things that turned them on, especially Culver, who was very, very gay. I tried not to hold that against him, and that was easy because ninety-nine percent of the time he didn't mean jackshit to me.

In the brief time I had known them, Finn and Rudy were usually trying to get laid. They showed zero interest in me and I in them, and the chicks they screwed were about my age. The fact that I didn't know those chicks made them seem older and wiser to me. I almost thought of being backstage, and sharing hotels, with male and female bimbos as some sort of education, as if it were some sort of preparation for real life.

Adnan had just turned eighteen. He was old enough to vote, drive a car and join the military. He was of age to be deployed to Iraq or Afghanistan and get killed or worse.

But he certainly wasn't old enough to be around sexual predators like Finn and Rudy.

I took a single step in their direction. Rudy grabbed me and asked, "Where you goin', girlfriend?"

I slapped his hand away and said, "Dude, I'm not your girlfriend. If you have a job for me, tell me and I'll do it. But if not, keep your hands to yourself. Understand?" I started over towards Finn and Adnan but Culver jumped in my way.

"What's the deal with that?" he asked. "Slappin' his hand away."

"Why aren't you over there with Adnan and Finn?"

He shrugged. "Adnan's a big boy. He can look after himself."

"Can he? Finn's getting a little friendly with him."

Culver smirked. "Maybe Adnan likes it."

Adnan and Finn left the suite together and I followed them. I watched as they disappeared into an elevator, and the car descended to floor eleven, the location of our suites.

I was amazed at the intensity of my feelings. Adnan was not my brother or boyfriend—for the past few weeks, he hadn't even been much of a friend.

I hurried back to my suite. Culver followed me, uninvited, because he had nowhere else to go. When I reached my door, he said, "I understand now. You're jealous."

That did it. I spun around and gave him what-for. I did so because he was right—I wanted Adnan, wanted him all to myself.

"Do you know why I'm here, doing this? Do you think my idea of summer fun is working as a fuckin' *roadie*, traveling all over the country with a bunch of no-talent assholes? I'm doing this because those Johnson jerkoffs revoked their scholarship, and they did that because of *you!*"

He said nothing. He just pointed to himself.

"Yes, you."

"I haven't done anything to you."

"Oh, but you have. Do you remember that afternoon in the caf? When we wrote that test? I sort of mouthed something to you. Remember? Well, they busted me for it, and Schloss said in private, 'Just blame Culver and I'll let you walk. You'll still have your scholarship, and you'll be giving me a good excuse to expel Chris Culver.'"

"He wanted to expel me? For real? How come?"

I shrugged. "Search me, man." Then I waited for him to say something like, "Don't sweat it— Stanford's not such a big deal after all." Then I could kick his ass and not feel so badly afterwards.

Instead, Culver said, "Well, why didn't you just tell Schloss it was all my fault? You would have been OK and my being kicked out of that school would have been no great loss for me. I didn't like it there anyway."

"My conscience told me what to do, so I did it."

Then Rudy appeared, his face as red as if he'd fallen asleep under a fourth of July sun.

"You," he shouted, pointing a long, meaty finger at me, *"are a lazy bitch. You're too busy kissing Queen's ass to do your job. You don't know the difference between a guitar and an amplifier. You probably can't tell your nose from your cunt—"*

Just then Culver stepped in and sent a loud, crisp slap to Rudy's face. "Chill, dude."

I blinked a bunch of times, not altogether believing what I had just seen. Rudy stood there, still crimson, the imprint of Culver's hand fresh on the left side of his stubbly face. The roadie, all shoulders, paunch and forearms, had been struck by a puny, rubber-wristed faggot; so why wasn't Rudy pounding the little queer into dog shit?

But the big man did no such things. He just stood there, mute and motionless, as if stunned with a Taser. In the time I had worked for him, I had always shrunk in the wimpiest way before his intimidation tactics. How could Culver be so unafraid of him? Maybe the kid *was* gifted, after all.

I could tolerate no more of this *mishigaas*. To be bullied again by Rudy, and defended by Culver? No thanks, no way. I gathered up what little remained of my dignity and strode away.

I walked up and down the stairs of the hotel a dozen times, my mind spinning. Rudy and Adnan, Rudy and me, Culver and me, Culver and Rudy—my universe had degenerated into chaos.

Rudy and Culver, I said to myself, could kiss my ass. But I cared deeply about Adnan; I always had, even though it had taken me seventeen years to figure that out. A long time ago I should have stopped caring about his goth look and loved him for the beautiful guy he was. I suppose I had only myself to blame. Even skinny, bespectacled Wizard had a crush on him—I should have realized that Adnan was hot stuff.

Christine, I said to myself, you are *such* a dummy.

By the time we entered high school, Adnan and I had become vastly different people. Yet he had never forsaken me, even when I gave him every reason to do so. Oh, I could be such a douche! Now that we had reached what I believed was the end of our friendship, I began obsessing over him. I could even hear his deep, mellifluous voice bouncing around inside my head.

I returned to our floor, and as I passed by Finn's room, I overheard raised voices, one of which was Adnan's.

"Don't touch me, dude," he said. "I'm not into…that."

I squared my shoulders and prepared to force the door open, but then I noticed it was ajar, so I merely pushed it open and bounded inside.

Maybe I'd expected to find Finn pinning Adnan to the floor, getting ready to sodomize my friend. Instead, I found them on the sofa, frowning at each other, the coffee table in front of them covered with Swarm paraphernalia.

"Get away from him!" I shouted at Finn.

"Get out of here, girlfriend," he shot back. "And keep your nose out of where it don't belong."

I did not get out of there. I upended the coffee table, sending Swarm items this way and that. Finn got up, but was unsteady, so when I planted my right foot into his middle and pushed him backwards, he went back and down.

"Get out!" I yelled at Adnan. "Run for it!"

He did so, but on his way out he snarled at me. For what? I wondered. I had just saved his rectum from a most unpleasant experience.

I got out of there too. As soon as I got back inside my own room, I found an envelope on the floor. I picked it up and had a look. It was from the laboratory to which we had sent the blood samples.

The DNA testing was a done deal.

But I was starting to think it didn't matter anymore.

CHAPTER 22

I slept very little that night. I started to realize that getting by on insufficient sleep was as much a fact of rock 'n' roll life as a taste for sex and dope.

Queen had made sure that I got my own room, and I felt grateful not to have to share my sleeping space with Rudy. He snored, groaned and farted all night, and was worse when drunk. His hangovers made him crankier than a hungry bear.

The letter from the lab confirmed that I was Queen's daughter. Surprise, surprise. Now I could go up to her, get the Stanford bucks and know that I had a wonderful future after all. Then I could quit this freak show called *Punk Off!* and go home.

The weird thing was, the notion of leaving this punk festival brought me no satisfaction whatsoever. I was the farthest thing from a punk rocker, and lacked the ability or inclination ever to become one. Yet, when I imagined going home to Mommy and Daddy, it just looked way too boring. At home, I was still Christine, the child I had always been. On the road with Swarm, the people around me seemed to consider me an adult.

But of course I had very little say in things after that incident with Finn. That would probably cost me my job and everything else. If, after being fired, I still wanted college money from Queen, I would have had to sue her or something, and I hated the idea of doing such a thing. My worst nightmare was spending the rest of my life working for my dad in his corner store, wasting my first-rate mind on the mundane details of running a humble little business. That freaked me out more than anything else.

I sat in my hotel room, staring for the longest time at nothing in particular, then did what I had always done when something I can't deal with gets right up in my face: I ran. Well, actually I walked at first, up and down the hotel's many flights of stairs. If I'd had roof access, I might have jumped, flapping my arms and wondering why I couldn't fly.

After partially exhausting myself on the stairs, I dashed through the lobby and out the front entrance. Downtown Green Bay was alive and thriving, but I was stuck too much in my own little hell to enjoy its vibrations.

Old ladies and suits frowned at me as I hurried past them on my race to nowhere and nothing. Maybe I thought that if I ran long and hard enough, I would find a place on Earth where they had the answers to all of my questions.

I ran till my lungs burned and my heart nearly exploded. I'd gone past churches and hospitals, office towers and bridges. When I finally came to stop and rest, absolutely nothing had changed. I was still who I was before, no wiser or better.

I looked around and saw a group of people standing at a corner a block or two away. They were oblivious to me, so I walked over towards them because I could no longer endure being alone. I needed those people, or someone else, to put an arm around me and say, "Oh, you poor baby. I pity you.

Life sure is unfair, isn't it?"

But who did I know in this cold, strange city?

I hailed a taxi, as always saving the receipt, and the driver took me to the *Punk Off!* fairgrounds. A dirt lane divided the site into halves, and on one half stood many, many filthy young people waiting to use the cramped, makeshift showers.

My destination was not the showers or the dirty people, but a dusty Geo Metro and its two occupants, the only people who gave a rat's ass about me.

Fortunately for me, the parking lot, such as it was, had pretty much emptied out, so the little old car was easy enough to spot. Their little tent was still there, and I saw Adnan packing things into the Geo Metro's trunk. He looked to me, in his tank top and jeans, like a *GQ* model. Nice big shoulders, small tight ass. I smiled at seeing someone from home.

He turned around and saw me. Instead of saying something nasty, he said, "Christine, are you OK?"

"No." I threw myself into his arms and bawled.

After a very long time—which may have been only a few minutes—I heard a sissified male voice. "Adnan, we're getting low on shit—" Then, "Wow! Is that *you*, Christine? You want me to go away?"

"No, stay," I said, pulling myself away.

"Looks like you two want to be alone," said Culver.

"That's not how it is."

"Oh, I hope you're wrong. Do you know how long I've been waiting for you two to hook up?"

Adnan waved him off. "Stop it."

"I just came by," I told them, "to say I'm quitting

147

Punk Off! and going back home to mind my old man's corner store."

"How come you're quitting?" Adnan asked. "Does it have something to do with me?"

I shook my head. "I had this idea of getting Queen Bea to pay for Stanford, but I can't do it. I'm no good at confrontations, and I really have no right to her money. She earned it, I didn't."

They both nodded. "So," Adnan asked, "is there anything we can do for you right now?"

"You can take me with you. I'm short on transportation and funds."

"Get in," Culver said. "Where's your shit?"

I pointed to my luggage. "Don't have to tie it to the roof. Last time—"

"Yeah, yeah." Then, "Sorry I fucked up your scholarship."

"You didn't do any such thing. You want to know who did that? It was Schloss, the principal. You have nothing to feel guilty about."

He said nothing, he just drove off.

Adnan turned to me. "Does Culver really think he was responsible for your losing that Johnson thing?"

"Yeah, and there's really nothing I can say that will change his mind. But it doesn't matter, anyway. Rich, beautiful college kids make me uncomfortable."

Adnan looked down at the mud. "If we're going to start throwing blame around, save some for me. I was the one who kept after you about tutoring him."

I almost laughed. Adnan, the guy who feared nobody, who had stood up to jocks and eyeballed them till they backed off, now wiped tears from his cheeks. Our school's punk-goth nihilist, who believed the whole shithouse of modern civilization should be torn down and thrown to the dogs…this person now wept for little ol' me.

"Don't cry," I said to him. "It's not as bad as all that."

But he cried harder and harder. Passersby stopped for a moment to gawk, so I smothered him in my arms as best I could, less to comfort him than to prevent him from throwing a full-blown tantrum. He fairly shuddered in my arms, so I looked for the first private place—his pup tent—and took him inside.

In the smelly darkness, I murmured, "Adnan—"

He gave me no chance to say anything more. He covered his mouth with mine. He slid his tongue down my throat and rolled over on top of me. He squeezed my breasts and moaned; or maybe I moaned. Maybe we both did—it was hard to tell.

Up till then I didn't think anything good could come out of my Stanford disaster.

Shows you how much *I* knew.

Culver was courteous enough to stay away all day, and I must say I scarcely noticed his absence. Adnan and I crawled out of that tent just long enough to use the toilets. We did stop bumping uglies long enough for him to apologize for being a dick, and I said I was sorry for being a bitch.

We had ended up in each other's arms mostly because I had been stripped of my status as a Young Libertarians hotshot and future Stanford student, and he had, literally, shed most of his goth persona. So we had done away with those things that had separated us, and we became one in a crusty pup tent somewhere in Middle America.

Naturally, neither of us knew how our relationship would turn out once we went back home and resumed our normal lives, but none of that seemed to matter as we lay there in that tent.

At around seven o'clock, Culver returned with a couple of deluxe pizzas and two six-packs of Coke Zero. As I picked the chunks of pineapple off my slice of pie and tossed them to the birds, I grinned at the thought that if food hadn't arrived, Adnan and I might have started eating the tent.

Adnan said to Culver, "You didn't have to bounce all day. You could have stuck around."

Culver giggled. "I just thought you two needed some quality time together. Besides, I wanted some quality time, too. I wasn't lonely."

Adnan frowned. "What's that supposed to mean? Have you found a boyfriend or something?"

"Affirmative."

"Anyone I might know?" asked Adnan.

"Could be."

"Then tell me, for fuck's sake!"

Culver winked at me and stuffed his mouth with pizza.

Adnan, with mock seriousness, pointed his finger at Culver. "After all the awful stories you've told me about your love life, something good happens and you don't tell me? What the fuck is up with that?" Then, "Spill it now or I'll beat it out of you."

Culver did something I had never seen anyone do when being bullied by Adnan: Nothing. He simply chewed on his pizza and stayed mute. Culver wouldn't let Adnan push him around. I greatly admired his backbone.

The three of us stood by the Geo Metro and

watched the last of the festival punks head to the next city. I think it was Detroit; we would hang out here for a few days and rejoin *Punk Off!* in Chicago.

My own future and plans were a huge question mark. All I knew was that I was hanging out with Adnan for the time being.

At Culver and Adnan's insistence, I slept with them in that tent, which was just big enough to fit two. Sleeping in the Geo Metro would have been even worse, so I squeezed into the tent, remaining on my side, staring at nothing in particular.

By morning, I figured that Swarm would know that I had split, and I wondered if any of them gave a shit. Certainly Rudy would be glad to see that I was gone, and I felt relieved that I would never see him again. Kitty Litter would need to find another gofer to fetch her nachos and Mountain Dew, and another roadie would be in charge of wiping the smudges off Maxie's drums.

As far as I was concerned, my summer adventure was a done deal. I'd wanted to use this road opportunity to get acquainted with my biological mother, but that would have happened by now. So I decided just to write off this whole experience and go home. I would work at Dad's store, buy lottery tickets and hope I won. My options had been reduced to that.

My life sucked *so* bad.

The three of us went nice and slow to Chicago. We pulled into a fancy roadside stop that had free wi-fi so Adnan could check his emails and generally diddle around online.

When we finally reached the Chicago site, we got the best possible piece of land—right next to the bathrooms and showers. Because we'd skipped the last show, everyone else from the tour was still in Detroit, so we were the first to reach Chicago. Colostomy would be onstage in the Motor City at that moment, getting the crowd worked up for the appearance of Swarm. Queen, backstage and out of sight, would be psyching herself up for yet another performance. Rudy would be darting this way and that, screaming, *"Where is that bitch Christina?"* as he, alone, prepared Maxie's prized drum kit.

At any moment the band would rip into "I Wanna Have Your Abortion." Longtime Swarm fans would imagine the song's brutal opening guitar riff the way Rings 'n' Things had played it. Personally, I heard Dina Dinner's riff—more raw and violent than Rings', or at least louder.

Dina's performances with Swarm had huge significance to punk fans, and on the Geo's crappy little radio we heard that Rings was suing Swarm for wrongful termination or something. Adnan and Culver went on and on about it during that daylong drive.

That Detroit gig was the only *Punk Off!* date I had missed, and while I was glad to be away from Rudy and the screaming masses, I felt I had let everyone down. After all, I had a job to do, and instead I decided just to goof off with Adnan and Culver.

I cuddled Adnan and tried to ignore Culver's buzz-saw snoring. After spending so many nights in big-city first-class hotels paid for the festival's organizers, I concluded that roughing it like this just didn't cut it.

Chicago, Illinois. The Second City. The Windy City. The place where I'd pull my panties and do my squats.

CHAPTER 23

As soon as the Detroit show ended, everyone hustled off to Chicago, and by late morning the site was no longer ours alone. Vast numbers of cars kept the Geo company, and the air was pungent with the smell of Safeway weenies sizzling on hibachis. I stood outside our tent and checked them out, admiring their camaraderie and spirit of community. They looked like spiky haired, punked-out freaks but laughed and joked like 'Sixties mellow-heads. One took a bite, decided he'd had enough, and passed the food to the next person. Nobody owned anyone or anything. I wondered what the Stanford folks would've thought of so much sharing and caring.

Ling, I said to myself, would *shit* at the sight of so many raggedy people who were not behind bars. I felt the same way, too, a few times, but once I decided they were harmless I could talk and listen to them and mostly enjoy their company.

At some point Culver disappeared for a while, and Adnan I retreated into the tent and did some more of that fun stuff we'd done earlier, just to make sure it was still fun.

It was. In fact, it was even funner.

It occurred to me that apparently I now had a boyfriend—who would soon go off to college and maybe meet someone better. Where did that leave me? To spend the next few decades working at

Daddy's store? I could do that, certainly, but somehow it lacked the appeal of spending four years at Stanford.

In truth, every time I contemplated my future beyond the next few days, I started having anxiety attacks. I wasn't even sure I wanted to go to the Chicago show with Adnan and Culver. I wanted to see Queen Bea strut her stuff once more time, but even that seemed kind of a bummer.

At first, I was unaware of the disorder, but as I woke up inside the tent the many voices outside sounded louder and more strained. Yells and shouts and raucous laughter were simply a part of *Punk Off!* life, especially now that virtually everyone who wanted to be there had arrived, and the site was packed. In a few hours, the show would begin; the competition for parking had ended and the battle had begun for a place to stand by the stage once the show began.

Adnan and Culver had buggered off without telling me their destination, or maybe they'd mumbled something about going to get groceries. So I pulled on my sweatshirt and Levi's and got out of the tent. Amazingly, the lineup for showers and toilers was almost zero, but quite a commotion was happening at the other end of the site. I wondered about that as I made the very brief walk to shit and shower.

When I returned to my tent with a clean body and empty bowels, the noise and excitement had intensified. A lot. Something very peculiar was going down.

I spotted Willie, one of my biker acquaintances. "Hey!" I called out. "What's the big deal?"

"She's *here*, baby! Can you dig it?"

"I can dig it!" Then, "Who's here?"

"Queen is here!" he yelled, beaming. "She's chillin' with us here in the camp! Come *on*! Let's go check her out!"

"For real?"

"Would I bullshit you?"

I hurried along with him, trying to keep my feet inside my flip-flops.

Queen was out here with the fans? That didn't sound like her at all. Dina Dinner was more that way, meeting and greeting and drinking her fans' beer. Queen had told me that she couldn't maintain her public persona—crazy, reckless, violent—in front of fans in a private meeting because she had gotten mellower and milder over the years. My guess was that someone had dressed up like Queen and was mingling with the fans who were buying her act.

But then I eyeballed her, tall, blonde, beautiful and dangerous as she walked here and there, followed by people who stayed several feet behind out of fear or deference.

Yes, she sure had that effect upon people.

Naturally, I saw her before she saw me. But once she did, she strode over to me as a mother might march up to a misbehaving child.

Maybe that was how she actually saw us. Maybe that's who we were.

"You," she said, pointing at me. "Do you have any idea of how many people have freaked out because of your absence? You have an obligation to us. Do you know how that makes *me* look when you just take off and don't tell anyone where you're going?"

Her voice was loud and overheard by many. They tittered or gasped. Queen Bea was pissed at me, and I suppose the onlookers wanted to see how long it would take her to kick my ass.

I wanted to retort, "When Rings collapsed on stage just a few feet from you, you didn't give a shit. When she had surgery, you were, like, 'Oh, well, too bad. Is Dina Dinner available to replace her?' So why are you showing so much concern about me?"

But I said no such thing. I did say, "Queen, Finn and I—"

She waved me off. "Finn is a prick. He can kiss my ass. But just because you had some kind of conflict with him doesn't mean you can just say, 'Fuck this, I quit.' You don't just run off and leave everyone wondering if you're still alive."

"I didn't know you cared," I muttered.

"What did you just say? Did I hear you right?" Her ice-blue eyes grew wide. *"Maybe I wasn't the one who fed and clothed you, but I'm still your mother!"*

She said plenty more, but *I'm your mother!* kept bouncing around in my skull.

Queen's full pink flips kept flapping, and my mind cleared enough for me to hear her shout, "I promised your old man that I would look out for you when we got on the road. Don't make a fool of me, girlfriend! You hear?"

I nodded and shrugged till my shoulders were sore. "Sorry. It's just that I thought Finn had fired me."

She spat on the ground. "That's what I think of Finn. If he fired you, I'm rehiring you. Are you going to stay on the tour or go home?"

"I'm with you."

Backstage, I got the impression that nobody had missed me. It was just, 'Do this, do that, kiss my ass.' So I did everything except kiss their asses.

Actually, my heart skipped a beat when Rudy sort of smiled and said, "Glad you're back." Maybe Queen had threatened to castrate him if he was rude to me.

My heart skipped another beat when I learned that Maxie Padz had found another caregiver for her precious drum kit. The kid's name was Aubrey, and I pitied him because I knew how anal Maxie was about her drums. When Aubrey dropped a cymbal, Maxie threw the kind of tantrum one usually sees when a little kid is told he can't have any ice cream.

Finn had hired a dietitian, a chick named Merritt who looked like a *Sports Illustrated* swimsuit model. He probably thought her boobs were natural; I could tell they were fakes. I saw Kitty working on a Cinnabon and licking icing off her lips as Merritt stood with her back to Kitty.

I saw someone else new backstage, a short, stocky suit with a manila envelope in his hand. He stuck the document in Finn's chest, who spread his arms and let the thing fall to the floor. The suit picked it up tried to give it to someone else. They had briefed me about him. The man, Irving, was a lawyer Rings 'n' Things had hired to serve the document—an injunction—to Swarm ordering the band not to perform without her. They had told *me* not to accept the envelope, either, because, nobody that I was, I was still considered a legal representative of the band, so if Irving handed the thing to me and I took it, he could say that Swarm had been served, and Swarm definitely did *not* want that kind of service.

Finn nodded at me and said, "Hey, girlfriend."

I sneered. "Stop calling me that. I'm nothing to you and you're nothing to me."

"You're less than nothing to me," he retorted. "If it was up to me, you'd be unemployed. You would have to buy your own ticket to this thing and you'd never get backstage."

"How did you survive the Nineteen-eighties?" I asked, wanting to change the subject.

He looked past me, and his face filled with the wistfulness of a man recalling long-gone good times. "You have no idea what it was like with Swarm in those days. Sex, drugs, rock 'n' roll! If there's a heaven we go to after we die, it can't be better than those parties from way back when. That was a crazy time to be young."

"You've come a long way, baby," I muttered.

Finn snapped out of his reverie. "Oh, and are *you* such a big fuckin' deal? I heard you were going to Stanford but you somehow you fucked that up, so now you're here, an eighteen-year-old big-nosed chick who's working as a roadie. Congratulations."

We had been speaking over the racket made by Colostomy as the band finished up. The crowd cheered for a few moments, then just applauded, then mostly went quiet.

This was the moment when Colostomy's roadies would break down their band's shit as fast as possible and I would help my crew throw together Swarm's equipment. As we did so, I got the feeling that this would be my last time. Maybe seeing a dozen or so of Chicago's finest near the stage made me think that.

Irving the lawyer stood talking to one of them, the

sergeant or lieutenant, and pointing at the injunction still in his hand. The boss cop shook his head a bunch of times, doubtless telling the legal eagle that the police couldn't enforce an injunction so long as it remained in Irving's hands. I chuckled at how many times I had seen the poor lawyer try to force the injunction on us in the past half hour.

The house lights went down and the crowd roared.

"Ladies and gentlemen—Swarm!!"

I can't say for sure, but I thought the band sounded even louder that evening. Maxie's drums had a *boom-boom-boom* resonance I hadn't heard before, and Kitty's bass made my bones throb. Dina Dinner played her guitar so violently that her fingers nearly bled.

And what of Queen? Maybe it wasn't the crazy 'Eighties anymore, but that evening she stalked the stage and cursed the unfair universe like an outraged teenager.

I took it all in, letting "I Wanna Have Your Abortion" slide down my throat as if it were sweet nectar. Up until that evening, I hadn't even liked that song, but now it was different—or maybe *I* had changed. After hearing it on my computer, in my own home, I had dismissed the song as just so much pointless noise. Later on, I had come to appreciate certain parts of it, but as I met the people who played it and—often in spite of myself—came to like them and respect their musicianship, such as it was. That night I liked the song, the singer, the lights and summer air, and the sheer pleasure of being part of a large gathering of people who were there to have fun together.

I had done it, I said to myself. I had become a punk. I wasn't altogether sure that was a good thing.

I stood backstage, watching as the other roadies and such monitored soundboards and fixed blown amplifiers and got ready to replace guitar strings once they snapped. Such emergencies were inevitable.

Then I saw him—Chris Culver—dancing in the wings as roadies rushed past him. Culver pumped his slim hips and ground his tush like a stripper. I wondered why he was there—no backstage pass hung from his scrawny neck. Right away I looked for Adnan but could not find him. I looked some more at Culver, who smiled at me, blew me a kiss and started swishing over towards me.

Then it happened, and it looked like a bad Marcel Marceau performance. Culver had taken maybe four steps in my direction before Irving the lawyer jumped in front of him and thrust the injunction into the chest of the one person backstage who did not know what it was and why he must refuse it.

"*Culver—no!*" I shouted, my voice rendered inaudible by Dina Dinner's guitar riff.

Culver frowned and shrugged as he accepted the document.

Then the world ended, sort of.

Irving signaled for the police, and out they came. They took out their nightsticks and started beating the bejesus out of the soundboard until the music went dead. A few of them surrounded Culver so that he wouldn't run away.

"*What the fuck!*" yelled Finn as he raced towards the cops surrounding Culver. "That kid is just hanging out here! He isn't one of us! He can't accept that injunction!"

Many of the countless thousands of people in the audience started booing, screaming and making obscene finger gestures. Some of them climbed onto the stage but the cops whacked them with nightsticks and pushed them back into the crowd.

From out of nowhere, Merritt, Kitty's dietitian, appeared. I watched her charge onto the stage and take out a folding knife.

"No! Don't!" I screamed, wondering why a dietitian would carry a big pocketknife. I flashed on an image of John Lennon's face as he was blown away by Mark David Chapman. Maybe that was Merritt's thing—to make her name in this world by killing Queen Bea.

My heart thundered in my ears as I struggled through the mass of cops, roadies and musicians wrestling with each other. Merritt ducked and dodged her way to the drum kit, and as I froze in disbelief, she slashed each of the drums. Merritt got everyone's undivided attention.

Maxie sure paid attention. I had never heard a human being howl in such horror and pain.

Merritt reached into a drum and pulled out a stack of bills half a foot thick. She reached in with the other hand and pulled out lots more.

The police forgot all about Rings and her injunction. Now they had a new thing to work on and plenty of questions to ask.

I stood there, staring and blinking and shaking my head. Why were the drums full of cash? Whose cash? As Finn had asked, *What the fuck?*

The cops busted us—Swarm, the roadies and other crew members. Me, too. They took us downtown and did their thing. That was how I met Detective Kelvina Barrow and her latex glove.

Truth is, I didn't know much about my vagina, especially that I could hide stuff in it. When she told me that I would have to squat, I burst into tears. I had been to the gynecologist many times, of course, but that was different. My gynie was a nice lady.

"Why are you picking on me?" I asked Detective Barrow between sobs. "It wasn't my money or my drums. I had nothing to do with this."

"I'm sorry, Christine," she replied. "But when we have a suspicious matter like this involving large amounts of cash, and officers are assaulted, we have to follow certain procedures."

"Oh." I guessed that when they saw all that cash sealed inside a drum kit, they would just assume it was all counterfeit or dope money or unreported income or…something.

So I went into that cold room, got naked and shivered as I did my squats till my thighs and lower back burned. I left that police station blushing, sweating and so disoriented that an officer had to lead me by the arm to the exit door.

I learned soon enough that Rings 'n' Things had nothing at all to do with this ordeal. Merritt, the nutritionist, was actually a private eye hired by Kitty Litter's ex to find out where Kitty had hidden her loot. Well, they found it.

As the tour traveled from city to city, Kitty would go to the bank and withdraw some of her money and stash it inside Maxie's drums. Once the punk festival began its European half, she would deposit her greenbacks in a Swiss account so that her ex couldn't get at it.

Kitty, at about five in the morning, told the cops about her money and plans for it while we were in the police station. She did so in order to keep her own panties on and legs together.

Swarm disbanded that evening, and they did so because Kitty spoke up about the money only when the other band members had been strip-searched and the police said to her, "Now it's your turn."

The disbandment happened in front of the cops. There was no yelling, screaming or fighting. Queen simply faced the other women and said, "I'm through. I don't want to do this any longer."

Finn said, "You can't do that! You have so many fans! You ladies have known each other forever! Plus, you've signed contracts!"

Queen shrugged. "Whatever, dude. It's all over. I'm going home."

I would have felt even worse about their breakup if the other ladies had tried to talk her out of quitting. But Rings had split, Maxie looked as if all she wanted to do was get into her SUV and drive back to suburbia and Kitty was totally obsessed with making sure her ex didn't get any of her money.

"The bitchiest band in the land" had gotten old and tired.

Queen and I took a taxi to our hotel, packed our suitcases and headed out to O'Hare. She bought herself a one-way ticket to LAX and got me one for home.

She seemed to be in a much better frame of mind, now that she'd told Swarm of her plans and was on her way back to Malibu to hang out and chill for a while. She smiled as I called my folks and asked them to meet me at the airport.

We sat in the VIP lounge and drank Fresca. "That cavity search we had? It wasn't the best I'd ever had. Some of them are kind of fun," she said, giggling.

I giggled, too, in spite of myself. "Being treated like a common criminal was a bummer."

She nodded. "Sorry you had to go through that. I guess your summer wasn't much fun, huh?"

"Oh, it was a *unique* experience. Getting to know you…"

Queen smiled. "Part of my plan for us was to spend more time together. Too bad that didn't work out. Still, I want you to remember that I'm your birth mother, We'll always be family to each other, and if there's anything I can do for you, feel free to ask."

My mouth dropped open. Was Queen saying, *Cut the foreplay; if you need money for Stanford, just ask. I won't say no*?

My brain seized up on me; I could not speak the one sentence she needed to hear. I just sat and stared at her, my face frozen as if by a stroke. Just then I heard the announcement for boarding of my flight. Unable to ask Queen for money, I got up, nodded goodbye and thought for a moment that Beatrix Potter Spurl, whom I had tried to shake down for many thousands of dollars, was the most beautiful person I had ever met.

"I'm not worthy of you!" I cried out. Then I ran off to board my flight.

CHAPTER 24

Swarm's sudden disbandment and withdrawal from the *Punk Off!* tour made news from coast to coast and beyond. A few million dollars in large bills were part of the news story. Maybe Maxie had hoped that the incident would escape the notice of her divorce-court judge. But no, it didn't.

The participation of Kelvina Barrow in this incident was considered trivial by everyone but me. Barrow starred in my nightmares for a while.

Punk fans everywhere were heartbroken at first to learn that Swarm was no more; to them, Swarm without Queen Bea was nothing. In fact, it was less than nothing.

But the *Punk Off!* organizers got smart in a hurry. As soon as Queen called it quits, they called the Bay Area and got another punk legend, Penelope Houston of the Avengers, to fill in as lead vocalist.

They trumpeted the news: "For the duration of the tour, punk sensation Dina Dinner will continue taking the place of Rings 'n' Things, and punk icon Penelope Houston will be the legendary band's new lead singer!"

The fans ate it up, including Adnan and Culver. Penelope Houston with Swarm! How could anyone beat *that*? My two friends attended the shows in the Northeast. Immediately after the Boston gig, they would head back home to get ready for college and their glorious futures.

I called Adnan, and while he sounded amped up about seeing Penelope Houston rock with Swarm, he showed some concern for me and my generally shitty state of mind.

"Can't you talk to Schloss and try to work something out? Is it too late to blame Culver for that caf incident?"

"Yes," I said, "it's too late. What's done is done. When you're fucked, you're fucked, and that's me. *I'm* fucked."

When I got back home, I made an appointment to see Rod Schloss. He'd opened his office a couple of weeks before the. The start of classes, so I got in to see him right away.

Mom was delighted to see me get off that plane and return home looking and acting much as I had before going to work for Queen and her gang. Actually, I wasn't the same old Christine—I was a new Christine, more mature and womanly, or at least not so bratty and girlish.

"I'm glad we're back together now," Mom said, as if I'd just been freed from kidnappers. She clearly wished to know nothing more about my experiences on the road, and I was quite happy to respect her feelings.

"So," Dad asked, "what's the deal with Stanford? Are you going?"

"Negative."

"What happened? Did you ask her? Did she say no?"

I shrugged. "I didn't ask. The more times the

chance came up for me to put the squeeze on her, the more I thought it was a despicable thing to do."

He frowned. "You know, your dorm room number came in the mail. I hope you can get your deposit back. I've set up a bank account for you so that you can get into some college next year."

I nodded thanks, but guessed that my future would include no college, not even Euphoric State. Instead, I would mind the counter at my father's corner grocery store, have a completely unfulfilling telephone relationship with Adnan and spend countless hours daydreaming of what might have been.

East Cupcake High School, as I liked to call it, was where I had spent the past four years. I disliked it because it was high school, and as I stood on its front lawn I regarded it much as a parolee would the prison in which he'd just done time.

I felt oppressed and sickened as I entered the building and walked towards the principal's office. I despised the school's musty smell and the loud voices that filled its classrooms. I knew that, wherever they were, Adnan and Culver wished me well, and I could feel their good vibrations in my limbs and soul. I only wished I could cast out Culver's psychic energy. I supposed he was a nice enough kid, but he had a remarkable talent for turning gold into lead. He would go off to college and we would never again speak to each other, although perhaps Adnan might relay updates to me about him, but I cared very little about that.

"So, Christine," Schloss said as we sat across from

each other in his office. "Did you have a nice summer?"

I nodded. "It was OK. I worked and traveled." Then, "I guess you know that I won't be going to Stanford after all."

"Yes, that's unfortunate. But you made that choice."

I sighed. The Spurl Girl wanted to fuck him up, but I was there to ask him for something, not antagonize him.

"Mister Schloss," I said, "I came here to ask you to take that black mark off my permanent record. This year is a write-off, but I'm making plans to apply to college for next year. As I'm sure you know, the schools I have in mind would turn me down the moment they learned of my black mark."

I expected him to say, "Sure. Fine. Done." Instead, he said, "Christine, you're asking me to commit an infraction to cover up *your* infraction. I can't do that."

"I committed no infraction! If anything, you wanted my assistance in expelling a student just because you were opposed to his sexual orientation."

The man waited a few moments. Then he said, "You committed an infraction. You got caught."

"OK, admit I mouthed something during the test. But look how much you've punished me for it! Isn't that excessive?"

I looked past him, out the window. I saw a light-blue sky with puffy white clouds drifting under a big bold sun. Everyone has his own idea of perfect weather; this was mine. "This has nothing to do with infractions and punishment," I continued. "It has to do with your homophobia and your unwillingness to put things right because that would mean admitting that you had done wrong in the first place."

His face clouded; he bared his teeth. "Just who the hell do you—"

At that moment the quiet of the day was broken by the roar of a motorcycle engine and the smashing of a window as the bike crashed into Mister Schloss's office. We dived for cover into a corner of the spacious room and covered our faces from the shards of glass flying every which way.

Schloss and I got up at the same time and shook the bits of glass from our clothing.

"Get out of here!" he shouted at the biker. "Are you crazy? Get the hell out of here!"

The bike skidded to a stop just a few feet from us. At first I wondered if its driver might be dead. But no; off came the helmet and its owner shook out her blonde hair.

"Hey," said Queen Bea.

"Didn't you hear me? Get out of here! I'm calling the police!"

"Oh, so you're the guy." Queen pointed at him. "You call yourself an educator of young people, huh? Since when has an educator kept fine young people out of our best schools? If I wasn't such a lady, I would kick all your teeth down your throat."

The principal took a few deep breaths. "You're going to prison for this."

Queen sat back on her bike. "Yeah? Well, it'll be headline news, and I'll drag you down with me. I'll spread rumors about how you're a pedophile who wants to stick his thing into cute boys."

Schloss snarled. "You do that and you're dead meat!"

"Really?" Queen got off her bike and took a step towards him. "Show me how tough you are. I wanna see."

He swallowed hard and stormed out of the room, his feet crunching the glass that lay on the floor.

Queen folded her arms and laughed. "I thought he'd never leave."

I asked, "What are you doing here?"

"Culver told me where you were."

I frowned. "But he's miles away with the tour."

"Rudy has a smartphone. He's still on the tour even though we're not. So do you. The world has become a small place."

"So you found out how to find me through Rudy, who got my whereabouts from Culver." I shook my head in total confusion. "So Rudy and Culver have met?"

She laughed. "Oh, more than that. They're lovers in love."

"Rudy the pussy hound likes boys, too," I muttered.

"Takes all kinds, huh?"

"Guess so."

She pointed at me. "How come you didn't tell me you lost your scholarship because of that creep I just scared off?"

"I figured it wasn't your problem."

"Well, you figured wrong. It very much is my problem. That's why I flew all this way and rented this Harley so I could come by and say hi to this principal. They'll stick me with the bill for crashing through this window and doing all this damage to this bike. Plus, your Stanford bills are gonna be a *bitch*."

My jaw dropped open. "Queen, I can't let you pay

those Stanford bills—"

"Too late. I've already written the checks. It's a done deal. But you have to promise me that you'll study your ass off and make top grades. Not everyone gets a Stanford education, so make sure you do it right."

I didn't know what else to do, so I threw myself at her for a nice big hug. But she stuck out an arm and shook her head.

"Nothing personal, Christine, but I'm pretty banged up right now. Might've broken a bone or two."

"Maybe," I said, "I should take you to the hospital."

"Or maybe," she retorted, "we should wait two minutes till the cops get here. They'll take me there."

Just then we heard the scream of a siren.

She was many miles from her Malibu home, cut and bleeding in a dozen or more places, minutes away from being cuffed and stuffed into a cruiser. Yet I had never seen her so at peace with herself and the world.

Queen Bea really cared about me. She really did.

"What can I do for you right now? I really want to help."

"Go home immediately. Pack your suitcases and head on out to Stanford. Freshman orientation week starts soon. Crack those books and finish at the top of your class."

We looked out the window and saw the police cars. The cops got out and pointed in our direction.

"But Queen, what can I do for you *right now*?"

She nodded. "Call Finn and run it down for him. He knows what to do in these kinds of situations

He'll get lawyers, arrange for bail—the usual bullshit. Now, bounce!"

"Yes, ma'am!" I fled out the door and down the hallway just as the cops arrived. I ran left and right until I reached the farthest exit of the school. I, Christine Slanz, former Young Libertarian, soon to be freshman at Stanford, should have been terrified but instead felt exhilarated as I scampered into the parking lot, got into my mom's car and zoomed off.

I, after all, was a Spurl, and we knew just what to do whenever shit happened.